D. Corisis

Spine-Tingling Tales to Read before Bed

This book is a work of fiction. Names, characters, and incidents are a product of the author's imagination or are used fictitiously. Any resemblance to any persons, living or dead, is entirely coincidental.

Copyright ©2025 Line By Lion Publications
 www.pixelandpen.studio
ISBN: 978-1-969677-09-0

Edited by K.I. Arkenau
Cover Design by @saritadraws

All rights reserved. In accordance with the U.S. Copyright Act of 1976, the scanning, uploading, and electronic sharing of any part of this book without the permission of the author is unlawful piracy and the theft of the author's intellectual property. If you would like to use material from the book (other than for review purposes), prior written permission must be obtained by contacting the publisher. Thank you for respecting author rights.

NO AI TRAINING: Without in any way limiting the author's [and publisher's] exclusive rights under copyright, any use of this publication to "train" generative artificial intelligence (AI) technologies to generate text is expressly prohibited. The author reserves all rights to license uses of this work for generative AI training and development of machine learning language models. Furthermore, Line By Lion Publications affirms that NO AI is used in the creation of our art. Support real artists!

For more information, email www.linebylionpublications.com

For my inspirational wife. She has nerves of cotton candy, but this horror anthology was her idea.

Table of Contents

Blooming Seduction

June 13, 1987

I encountered a strange plant on my excursion today. It was in a narrow gully, near the mouth of a cave where a creek originated. I never would have found it had I not slipped down the side of the muddy trail. Normally, I wouldn't dare take a specimen from the wild, but this plant… I just couldn't resist!

It's unlike anything I've seen, definitely not native to the area. The bud is roughly the size of my fist and stands several inches off the ground on a stalk about two inches thick. The bud is incredibly dense; roughly the same feel as a softball. Given the plant's mass, I assumed its root system would be well-established, but a gentle tug proved its root ball to be relatively shallow. Vines crept away from the base with a diameter of roughly one meter. Those farthest away vanished into the surrounding rock which broke away easily. I did what I could to preserve them during transportation. Few survived by the time I was back to my car. Those that remained were dried and falling off once I was home. I couldn't bring it inside fast enough, just to examine the plant in all its glory.

Glossy dark greens decorate its outward appearance with luxurious vibrancy. I can make out six seams running down the side of the bud with hints of dark purple and red.

Perhaps it's close to flowering? The stem is rigid and inflexible, colored with streaks of dark brown. I was careful with the remaining roots when replanting.

I am still determining what species it could be. The presence of vines, along with the shape of the bud, drives me to guess some form of Clematis. However, the size is far too large for such a species of flower. Possibly some undiscovered carnivorous plant? Although given its dimensions, I am surprised how the species has managed to avoid discovery for so long. Perhaps it's a unique hybrid or unseen mutation; maybe a migratory bird deposited the seed. Only time will tell. Once it blooms, I should be able to ascertain more.

June 14, 1987

I couldn't decide where to put her. Without more information, I don't want to risk placing her pot in an unfit environment. Granted, no setting would be catastrophic overnight, but nowhere felt...befitting. Her jewel-like exterior has absolutely captivated me, and I find myself unable to be apart. In the end, I placed her on a south-facing windowsill in my bedroom. Being on the second floor, there should be plenty of sunlight. I could always bring in a UV lamp if necessary. I would hate to let her out of my sight when I know so little about her.

Gus, on the other hand, is quite displeased by his new window mate. He still has his full cat bed attached to the glass, but seems unwilling to share any of his space with our new guest. I made sure to shower him with treats and give him plenty of attention. In no time, he was purring once more. He knows more than anyone how enthralled I can become with my horticulture; he also knows I would never choose a plant over my beloved friend. I did have to shoo him away from trying to knock the mystery plant to the ground. I will have to keep a watchful eye on those two.

But the good news is she's taken to her pot well! Her roots seem strong and her green color is more vibrant than ever. I could watch it gleam in the sunlight for hours. Even better, the bud has grown larger! Only slightly so, but enough to be noticeable. Bringing some of the bark and moss from the cave's mouth was the right choice; she couldn't be happier.

I will continue making constant observations.

June 15, 1987

She opened today! I awoke to the sound of Gus growling. I was surprised to see him huddled against the opposite window corner glaring at her. Perhaps there was a scent he wasn't fond of?

Oh, she's absolutely stunning. As I suspected, her bud opened into six lobes. Each unfurled into a thick triangular slab. Their curves remind me of rolling waves. At their largest, the petals are just over an inch thick and covered in silvery hairs. They all sway at the slightest movement in the air.

The interior is colored with striking reds and purples laced with prominent veins leading into a dark center, speckled with bright pink dots. There is mucus running over the petal surfaces that have begun dripping onto the windowsill. It smells of intense lemon. I suspect this is the cause of Gus's displeasure.

There is a single pistil rising from the center like a finger.

A group of four stamens encircle it, like dancers around a pole. They moved slowly like tentacles, but this must have been due to the breeze from my open window. Even with this new development, there was still something far more exciting.

Bugs.

There were empty insect husks tangled in the tiny hairs. Anything fleshy had been dissolved. I also found a small skull belonging to a snake. Given her size, it's not out of the realm of possibilities to imagine even a modest-sized serpent becoming trapped upon her closing. The body would have been left to the elements outside of her trap to be carried off by some other predator.

Now I know she's carnivorous. A big step in the right direction. Immediately, I rushed to the pet store and bought a bag of crickets. Gus was angry upon my return, but he will have to learn to live with her.

One by one I dropped the bugs into her waiting petals. She didn't close right away like a venus fly trap. In fact, she remained motionless, the crickets only becoming stuck in the mucus and entangled in the hairs. Only when I had deposited nearly twenty insects did she come alive.

There was a leisure to her movements. No sense of urgency. She knew her prey was already trapped with no hope for escape; why rush? Like a finale, I watched her lobes curl together before meeting at the top, once more sealing her beautiful colors away from the world.

That was probably the best meal she's ever had.

June 17, 1987

I can't believe how fast Mary is growing. In only two days, she's sprouted a mess of vines overflowing my windowsill. Their immediate purpose doesn't seem to be for drawing in water. Initially, I thought it might be time to move her into the greenhouse, or even the outside garden. In the end… I just couldn't bear not having her beauty in my bedroom. Waking up to the sun shining on her green surface is simply magical.

Freeing her vines to do as they please was the answer. Some have begun peeling the paint. Several are already deep into the drywall. It's unlike anything I've ever seen. Mary's vines have a certain…mobility to them. When I enter the room, I can see them tense. Some use their ends to search the open air like curious eels. It didn't take long to realize they were following my location. I suspect there are microscopic hairs detecting changes in air currents that alert her to any nearby movement.

Mary opened again this evening, far earlier than I was anticipating. Even the fastest of carnivorous plants take at least a week to dissolve their dinner. But when Mary opened up, sure enough, those twenty crickets were no more than hollow shells.

She was hungry and eager for more. I happily obliged with another healthy serving until she closed again. It took over thirty crickets this time. When closed now, she's larger than both of my fists combined. I will have to replant her soon at this rate, with something prepared for the next several stages of her growth. If I don't, her creeping vines may not allow me to do so without dramatic pruning.

I would never dare wound her in such a way.

<u>*June 18, 1987*</u>

I attempted to replant her this morning. Everything had to be done in my bedroom as her thickest vines couldn't be removed from my walls without being severed. Some had managed to dislodge my trim from around the floor. To mar such beauty would be unthinkable, so her transplant was done in place. I wanted to do it while I knew there was no risk of her opening. Considering the meal from last night, she would be occupied for a while.

I was given quite the start when I grabbed her stem and gently pulled her roots from the pot. Most of them held firm to my wall like tethers mooring a ship, but those that released writhed like tentacles trying to grab onto anything they could. I was initially frightened to see a plant acting like a defensive octopus, but when they wrapped around my arm, I felt something.

We made a connection in that moment. She knew I was taking care of her and wanted only the best. Every little hair and bristle stung my skin as her vines tightened around me, but I didn't care. I wanted her to know there was nothing to fear. That I only had love and adoration for her. That I knew she was alive.

By the time I was setting her into her new pot, my hand was throbbing and purple from how tightly her vines had coiled. Green mucus ran from her head while I packed bark around her roots.

She ended up breaking the skin on my arm. A rough edge on the vine sank too deep into the soft underside of my forearm puncturing a vein. I hadn't even realized it had gotten to that point. A warmth spread between my skin and her vines until a small trickle of red ran down their lengths. I was about to rush to get a bandage, but then she opened.

Oh, what an incredible display of beauty.

Mary's trap blossomed into a steaming scene of half-digested crickets. I could smell the decay and see the soup she'd been enjoying as it ran out of her and into the putrefying bark. It looked like I'd opened a dishwasher before it was ready.

It didn't take me long to realize what had driven her to give up the meal. Her vines loosened. I could almost see her petals pulsating with anticipation as I brought my wounded arm to hover over her. My arm had a mind of its own. It knew what Mary wanted.

Much to her delight, I was generous with my donation. I allowed my vein to empty enough blood to coat her petals in crimson. Only when she closed once more, my essence mixing with her own in swirls of red and green, did I allow myself to pull away.

Gus was glaring at me from across the room when it was finished, but I paid him little mind. Mary was happily repotted, her vines were intact, and above all, I had found a connection with a plant I never thought possible.

For a moment I stared at her, taking in what I had just done. I watched a trail of viscous slime run down her side as she began digesting my blood. I'll admit that my mouth watered. If she was willing to try a taste of me, why could I not grant her the same?

The green fluid was surprisingly warm and coated my finger like syrup. It reeked of citrus, cricket, and raw meat, but I wanted to try it all the same. I *had* to try it. Gus watched as I licked the substance.

It was rank. Rancid. Putrid with decay. I nearly gagged but was taken aback by a delightfully fruity aftertaste that overwhelmed my senses. Mary continues to surprise me in every way. My throat burned for hours after the initial flavor, but it was worth it for the lingering bliss that came after. I went back several more times before I had to force myself to stop partaking in her juices.

She wasn't just carnivorous. She was eating her way into my heart.

<u>June 21, 1987</u>

If crickets are wood, my blood is gasoline. Mary's growth has exploded since being repotted. I can barely keep up! Her vines grind as they creep longer and thicker. It keeps me awake at night, like a room of dripping faucets. She's speaking to me. Begging for attention.

Her trap is growing several inches per day with the new diet. When closed, it's larger than my head. When open, it looks like a flowering umbrella of veins and alien membranes. I would be intimidated if I weren't so enthralled. She's managed to attach herself to the wall with a stem several feet in length and getting longer every day. There's a strange comfort in seeing Mary looming over the room with her petals open, like some kind of floral spotlight watching my every move.

Her thirst knows no end. She's opening up to feedings three to four times daily. My arm doesn't have time to start healing before I need to open myself up again. I'm making sure to take precautions and sterilize the razor beforehand. The occasional dizzy spell isn't too difficult to handle, but an infection is the last thing I want. Especially when it could affect Mary's health. The thought of filling a spray bottle with my blood would have been an outlandish thought in the past. Now, it's a convenient way to mist her lobes; she's so high up the wall that trying to hold my dripping arm over her would be fruitless. Watching her tiny hairs dance and bristle to collect her meal makes my heart throb. The entire corner of my room, now covered in vines, dances with her enjoyment like a living wallpaper.

Gus won't dare go near her anymore. He only comes close enough for attention when I step outside to tend to the garden. With so much of my blood being devoted to Mary, I can only work in the sun for a few minutes before needing a breather. He always jumps right into my lap like he used to. I guess the citrus scent really is getting to him. Poor thing. I realize I've been spending an inordinate amount of energy on Mary, but soon her growth should level out and things will return to normal. Gus understands. Still, it was nice to share some quality time with him again. I only brushed him off when I saw Mary open up through the bedroom window, ready for another feeding.

June 25, 1987

She broke out of her planter this morning. I awoke before daybreak to a great explosion only to find the pot shattered and molding bark spread across the floor. Mary's roots consumed my window with their newfound freedom. I panicked for a moment and attempted to remedy the situation, but they were steadfast after only a few minutes given to them. I don't think I could have moved them if I wanted to. She clearly wanted to be free of her ceramic walls. Who am I to stop her?

The vines have consumed most of my room. I can't walk on Mary's side anymore without disturbing them. The fissures in the drywall might anger me if she wasn't so beautiful. Interestingly, the thickest of the vines have sprouted flowers of their own.

Like Mary, these are a mystery to me. They are five-pointed and dark red, but far less meaty than their mother. They remind me a little of starfish, both in appearance and movement. If I watch them closely, I can see them swaying… Slowly opening and closing… As if they could crawl off their vine and explore the world… I'll admit it's a little unsettling. I had a nightmare recently, where I found one latched onto my ankle with spikes gnawing into my achilles tendon.

Mary consumes all of my time now. I can barely afford to do anything else. My energy is so sapped from feeding her my blood, that if I'm not tending to her, I'm sleeping. It's strangely comforting to sleep in a room that's so taken over by her vines. Like our own little grotto. And they're always different! Never arranged in the same pattern.

She can't climb any higher at this point. Her flower has come to rest in a high corner of the room with a petal span of over five feet. The main stem looks more like a utility pipe running along my wall. It's thicker than my thigh, and lined with veins that pulse and help deliver nutrients all over her body. A part of me wonders if her vines have managed to crack open a water line in the walls to sate her thirst.

I think she's very happy up there, although her mucus is leaking onto the floor and creating a nasty pool of sludge. Sometimes I feel like I can see her flower breathing. The effect is especially apparent when her petals are closed. Slowly, her bud will expand out and contract back in.

I cannot wait to see what comes next.

June 30, 1987

Gus has been missing for three days. His litterbox has gone unused. I haven't heard his usual cries for dinner. It wasn't until this morning that I actually started wondering about the last time I saw him. I think it was two days ago, but it could have been more. I've been so preoccupied with my beloved, that he completely slipped my mind. More than likely, we're better off without him. He hated Mary, and it was causing tension in our relationship. It took me forever to get the clumps of fur removed from her vines.

In other news, Mary had a magnificent surprise waiting for me.

It was downstairs. I hadn't ventured down there in several days. Why would I? Everything I need is on the second floor. If I get hungry, my beloved's nectar is more than sustaining. I've come to long for the rancid flavor. I almost wish the sweetness didn't follow.

But back to Mary's surprise. When I went downstairs to check for Gus, I found the backdoor completely blacked out. It was Mary's vines. My beloved's creeping embrace. She was cascading down the back wall of my house, like an emerald waterfall. She must have escaped the confines of my house days ago. The tentacle-like tendrils reacted to my presence on the other side of the door. They tapped on the glass like drunken bees trying to get at me. Even better, her glorious red flowers were everywhere. They adorned my backyard like ornaments on a Christmas tree. They curl and grasp at any movement in the air, no doubt capturing passing bugs and digesting them. Now my neighbors could take in her stunning beauty as well. But her main body, that man-sized blossom taking up a significant portion of my bedroom, was for my eyes only.

I didn't want to open the sliding door and risk disturbing Mary's vines. Gus couldn't have gotten out there anyway. Last I remember, he was inside and I couldn't recall the last time I'd opened the door. I was able to peer through some gaps between my beloved's vines. All across my yard...the grass, my garden, along the fence, my hedges; I could see small fist-sized buds.

I was wondering why my yard had been so quiet the last few weeks. Not a sound out there at night save for her creaking vines. So peaceful.

Mary knows just what I need.

July 1, 1987

Pain. Incredible, intense, sharp pain. Sadly, I reacted too fast. I wish I had known it was Mary sooner, I would have left her be!

I woke up this morning with several of her vines growing under my toenails. Some thicker limbs had wrapped around my ankles while I slept, presumably to keep me from moving. But the moment I roused, I accidentally ripped out her tiny needle-like vines. My big toe was the worst; the nail was torn halfway off after her vines had ingrained themselves to my nail bed. I was left bleeding all over my sheets.

Watching my love's vines scramble to soak themselves in the growing pool of my blood helped calm my nerves, but I still felt deep regret. Mary was only hungry, and desperate for more food. Am I not feeding her enough? I should have known after her vines had engulfed my bed. Next time, I'll be more careful so I don't break her tender hands.

If she's hungry, I'm here to feed her.

July 5, 1987

I've stopped leaving my bed. It could have been a day since I last left, or three. I'm not sure. I just can't bear to damage Mary's work. Her vines engulf me and the mattress now. I'm no prisoner, I want to be with her. Wrapped in her. Coddled and cradled by her arms and the warm caressing touch of her flowers.

Yesterday was the Fourth of July. Normally, I don't care much for fireworks, but this time… Oh, they were exquisite. Every burst of color illuminated my room and played across Mary's dripping face. Yellows and greens danced over her purples and reds. Her flowers almost seemed to burst open with every pop in the sky, basking in the sudden glow. The explosions of light cast shadows through the curtain of vines. They covered my room in their writhing, snake-like dances.

I should mention that I've given my feet to her. My nails are gone, all popped off like bottle caps. The pain was mind-numbing, as I felt her vines slowly digging their way into my unprotected flesh. It is still excruciating, but it's worth it to have her satisfied. I believe she's even made her way into my lower calf muscles. It's odd feeling her smaller vines under my skin and squirming their way up my legs. Sometimes a vine will tug on one of my tendons and flex my foot, causing my dried-out skin to crack. She explores my body more every day. She can do as she pleases.

I couldn't leave this bed now even if I wanted to.

July 7

Writing is difficult. She's everywhere. By the time I move to turn a page, I must break new vines from my arm to do so. I can barely breathe from the foliage wrapping around my torso.

I'm taking breaks between writing. Staying awake is difficult.

She's invaded my abdomen. It started at the navel and spread from there. She's inside of me. I can feel her in my muscles and between my sinews. I am sure I look grotesque. I noticed my blood has turned a sickly brown.

Mostly numb. Things snap when I move, and pierce if I move too much.

My body is her body. I am happy to give myself to her.

I stare into the darkness of her flower. It takes up my entire wall. Thorns have sprouted on the outsides of her petals. In the darkness they look like teeth. There has been knocking at my front door. Maybe the HOA is complaining about Mary's growth. Let them. My beloved's jungle is too much for anyone else to handle.

July 3

Not hungry. Skin is wondrous shades of green. Vine pumps nectar into stomach. There has–

Shouting outside sometimes. Loud knocks at door. Don't care.

Vines between ribs. Hurts to breathe. Don't want to disturb her.

She is so precious to me.

If something happens, feed Mary. I don't want–

<u>*Night*</u>

I am warm

Mary is bliss

About <u>*Blooming Seduction*</u>

Plants creep me out. Especially the big ones. A lot of people who read this one say, "It reminded me a lot of Little Shop of Horrors*!", to which I say, "Yes! Because Audrey II was terrifying!" That scene from* Jumanji*, where the giant carnivorous plant comes out of the fireplace and tries to pull the little boy into its mouth, also played a key role. To this day, I can't stick my hand into any plant's leaves without thinking about that scene. Harvesting things like pumpkins, tomatoes, or watermelons is not a calming* *chore.*

There could be a deeper meaning in this story if you look. Maybe it's about obsession and how it can consume our lives. Maybe it's about depression, and its ability to drain every bit of our essence until there's nothing left but a husk. If this story spoke to you on a metaphorical level, I'm glad. For me, I just wanted to put my fear of plants on paper and make other people feel that same anxiety for a few pages.

Gate C12

A rush of industrial air conditioning brought welcome relief when Mark entered the bustling Seattle airport. The sun was warm in the late afternoon, with not a cloud in the sky to block its rays. Once he managed to reunite with his wife, he would be happy to enjoy a gentle walk in the sunset with her hand interlaced with his.

Several days have passed since she'd flown to Montana for her sister's baby shower. From the sound of things, it had been the usual trip, laced with family drama and frustration. A bundle of flowers would help lessen his wife's fatigue when she passes through the security gates.

The usual crowd of people were gathered around the security area. After checking a teleprompter, Mike confirmed that his wife's plane had in fact touched down several minutes prior. Any minute now he expected her to walk through the automatic doors.

Weary passengers soon approached in a steady stream. Mike scanned the heads in search of his wife's tell-tale ponytail.

"Aww, for me? You shouldn't have!"

Mike glanced at a passing elderly woman as she smiled and motioned toward his flowers. He returned her grin. "They're all yours if my wife doesn't want them!"

"I'll hold you to that!"

They exchanged a final smile before she continued on her way. Mike was certain he hadn't missed his lover, but as the disembarking crowd thinned to only stragglers, he wondered if she had managed to slip by.

Being the last to get off a plane was hardly something to panic over. Mike decided to wait patiently. Reunions blossomed around him as families became whole again, and he wondered if maybe one day his own grandchildren might race to greet him at the airport. Such a reality felt a lifetime away.

Several more groups of passengers passed through security. Still there was no sign of her. Nervous, Mike pulled his phone from his pocket. There was nothing waiting; no text message asking his whereabouts, and no missed calls explaining some baggage problem.

He assumed she'd stopped at the bathroom, or maybe a particularly good coffee from a cafe had ensnared her into waiting in line. Regardless, Mike was certain he would see his wife stride through the doors any second, no matter the nervous anxiety that may have been bubbling within his gut.

Vibration from Mike's phone released all of his tension when he saw his wife's photo on the screen. He answered quickly, already feeling his worry wash away.

"Hey! I'm waiting outside security! Where are you? I was starting to–"

The line was full of static and garbled sounds. Patches of frantic words came through.

"–ike?... Are–... I can't–"

Mike furrowed his brows. "Laura? You're breaking up… I can't understand you…" He turned around, looking toward baggage claim. "Did you sneak past me?"

The static cleared, although her voice still sounded distant. "Mike? *Mike?*" Her tone gave him pause. There was deep worry and panic in Laura's voice.

Calmly he asked, "Can you hear me? I'm waiting–"

"I… *There's no one here!*" she interrupted. Heavy

breathing came through the phone, as if she were trying to catch her breath. *"There's nobody here!"*

Such claims puzzled Mike. Shifting his gaze, he inspected the throngs of people going about their business in the terminal. It was hard to believe an airport of this size could ever be empty.

Mike blinked. "Huh?"

"The airport, Mike! It's empty! Just...*empty!* It's completely abandoned! *Where are you?*" Laura's voice came through the phone with an echo, as if she were talking in a cavern. It carried a fluttering panic that made her words race.

"I don't understand… I'm at security. Where are you?"

A frustrated scream responded, *"At security!"*

Silence followed as Mike was taken aback by her outburst.

"S-Sorry," Laura said. "I… I'm really scared. This isn't one of your practical jokes, is it?"

He paid close attention to the people walking by, none were his wife. "I'm not sure what you're talking about. I'm sitting in a chair waiting for you to come out of security. Same place I always meet you."

"I'm *at* security, Mike…" Nervous sounds of panic came through the phone. He recognized them well and knew Laura must have been biting her fingernails. "I'm standing right in front of where you usually sit! I'm telling you, the place is *empty!*"

Mike paused. "Are you at the right airport?"

"THERE'S ONLY ONE SEATTLE AIRPORT!"

"I-I know! I'm just saying if you're at security, and I'm at security, and we can't see each other… then we're not at the same place."

Distressed groans came through the receiver.

"Something is wrong... Something is wrong here, Mike! There isn't even any music playing over the speakers! The halls are just empty! S-Some are completely dark!"

He could tell Laura was close to breaking down. "Ok, let's take a breath. What's the last thing you remember?"

"I... I was on the plane. I fell asleep after we took off. When I woke up, the plane was sitting at the gate. There was no flight crew, though! The pilot, the stewardesses, everyone was gone! I grabbed my carry-on and ran out of the gate because I thought I might get in trouble! But the entire airport was just...*dead!*" Her voice fell to a shaking whisper. "*Why is it so quiet?*"

"And you're *positive* it's the Seattle airport? SEATAC?"

"YES! I'm staring right at that stupid sculpture we always make fun of! The one of the frog with six legs!"

Her claim gave Mike pause. Looking down the hall, less than a dozen meters away, was the art piece in question. "Yea... That's a unique one..."

A shuddering crack came through the phone, making Mike recoil in shock. "What was that?"

"There's a thunderstorm outside... It's been raining since I woke up."

"It's eighty-five degrees and sunny... Are you sure you're in Seattle?"

Silence filled the void.

"Laura? You there?"

"Do you really think I don't know what Seattle looks like?"

"Well I was just–"

"I've lived in Seattle my whole life, Mike. I *know* what SEATAC looks like."

It was Mike's turn to create a pause.

Sighing, Laura's voice responded low and fearfully, "Sorry. I'm sorry. I'm just... Scared. This makes no sense."

A thought crossed his mind. "Wait, are *you* pranking *me?*"

There was a pause. Mike could feel her eyes narrowing and her nostrils flaring. "*Yes*, Mike. You caught me. I just got back from a weekend at my *very* pregnant, *hormone-riddled* sister's house, and thought to myself, 'You know what would be funny? I should act like I'm at a different airport.'" Laura huffed. "Gee, Mike, can't get anything by you, can I?"

"Alright, alright! Just checking!"

Laura grumbled amid static crackles. When composure partially returned, she said, "I'm going to go check something."

"What?"

"My flight status."

Mike approached his own monitors. "Mine says your flight arrived on time twenty minutes ago."

The resulting silence wasn't comforting.

"Laura?"

Slowly she said, "Mine says 'Diverted: See Attendant'..."

Mike strained his ears to listen through the phone as people talked around him. "Yours says diverted?"

Frantic, she exclaimed, "What attendant? What attendant, Mike? There's nobody here! The desks are empty! *This whole damn airport is a ghosttown!*"

The bouquet's wrapping crinkled in his fidgeting hand. "Hey, hey...! It's alright! Take a breath. There has to be *someone* around, right? Are the lights still on?"

"Y... Yea... Some of them, at least... The ones that aren't broken."

"And someone had to land the plane, right?"

"I guess..."

"So somebody has to be there. Maybe they moved the plane to an unused part of the airport while you were sleeping and didn't see you."

"I know where I am, Mike! I recognize it!"

Trying to keep her calm, he insisted, "Let me go talk to an attendant and see if they can help. I'm sure there's a logical explanation."

"Please hurry!" Laura sounded as though she were looking over her shoulder every few seconds. "All I can focus on are my own footsteps! It's so quiet, I can't hear myself think! I'm starting to imagine that I'm hearing things around corners!"

Mike made his way to a customer service counter. As far-fetched as her story sounded, Laura's description conjured frightening scenarios in his head. Some of SEATAC's hallways stretched over a thousand meters. It would be terrifying to stare down a desolate hallway only to see some unknown creature run across the other end. He didn't dare share such a ghoulish thought out loud.

Reaching a service representative, he told Laura, "Ok, I'll be right back! Hang tight!"

A woman behind a computer grinned as he approached. "Hello, sir. What can I help you with today?"

Mike scratched his head. "Well, uh… This is going to sound weird, but…is there another one of these airports?"

The customer service woman cocked her head. "I'm sorry?"

"Like another SEATAC, but unused?" Mike blushed from the ridiculous question.

Taken aback, the woman replied, "No, sir… This is the only SEATAC."

Confused anxiety made Mike tap his fingers on the counter. The flowers were starting to wilt. Of course he knew this was the only SEATAC, but his wife wouldn't be acting this way for no reason. "Can you check my wife's flight then, please? Flight 3773 on United… It landed but I haven't seen her yet."

"Certainly. One moment please."

Her fingers clicked and clacked away on her keyboard. The suspense was a sauna around Mike's head.

Finally, she responded, "Looks like it did touch down about twenty minutes ago… Everyone was accounted for and disembarked the craft. That particular plane is currently boarding for a flight to Boise. My system shows there were no passengers with connections on that flight, so she had to have left the craft."

Mike chewed his bottom lip in frustration. He'd only found more questions and still his wife continued to only exist on the other end of a phone call. "Ok, thank you."

"Let me know if there's anything else I can do for you!"

Stepping away, Mike returned to his call. "Laura?"

The fear was still prevalent in her voice. Electronic crackles and fissures split her words. "And? What did they say?"

"She said everything looks normal. A flight to Boise is boarding it right now. Everyone got off the plane after it landed."

"Well I obviously didn't because I was asleep! Did you ask her why the airport is abandoned?"

"It's not abandoned! There are a hundred people around me!"

" I haven't seen another person in over an hour! My voice is echoing through this place like a–" Her voice cut off.

Mike's heart jumped into his throat. "Laura?"

"Shh!" she hissed.

A sharp, distant warning sound came through the

receiver with Laura's voice.

"What was that...?" she asked, speaking softly. "I hear something. It sounds like an alarm..."

Mike grew cautious. "Well don't go near it."

"Are you crazy? Maybe it's someone who can get me out of here!"

"Laura! We–"

"There it is again! Just hang on. It's close."

The sound echoed with her voice through the desolate airport. Keeping quiet, Mike listened to her breathing as she hurried to find the source of the sound. It was familiar to him, though he couldn't place its origin.

Her voice made him jump when she announced, "Found it..."

"What is it?"

"It's... It's the baggage claim warning... Like when the bags start coming down onto the belt? Only..."

Mike didn't like the wavering tones in her voice. "What's wrong?"

"There are *mountains* of suitcases here."

"Huh?"

"Just... heaps of bags, Mike. Like they've been piling up over years... Decades, maybe! I–" A gasp came through the phone after a loud thud. "There's my bag!" Hearing her run and stumble over several objects, Mike listened intently. "It's definitely mine! This is so weird... No one else's came out... But this is a good sign, right? This means *someone* had to be around to unload it from the plane!"

Mike was too busy weaving between throngs of people to reply right away.

"Mike?" Laura asked.

"Hang on, I'm going to baggage claim."

Arriving at the rows of conveyor belts, Mike scanned the LED screens for one that matched Laura's flight number. He found it near the end. As he feared, the belt was empty.

"Your bag isn't here," Mike said.

"I know, because I just grabbed it."

"But you're not here either!" The situation was eating away at his stomach. The longer her absence dragged on, the more he feared something malevolent might have found his wife. "Can you look at the other suitcases? Do any of them have a name tag? Anything helpful?"

Laura was reluctant. "I… guess… It's really creepy standing around with all of this luggage though. I feel like I'm not supposed to see it…"

He listened to her crawl over several in search of a tag. Finally, she called out several names. "Uhhhh, Marilyn Pope? Zack Campbell? I've never heard of them. There are a lot more tags though."

Mike's heart was racing. "That should be enough. Hang on."

He took the phone away from his ear and opened a web browser. Searching for the first name made his heart sink. Searching for the second made him feel sick to his stomach.

His hand shook when he replaced the phone to his ear. "Those are names of missing people."

"Y-You're just trying to scare me. That's not funny, Mike. I don't appreciate–"

"I'm not joking. Marilyn Pope went missing in 2003,

after a flight from California. Zack Campbell has been missing since 2015. I just found several articles about them!"

Laura responded in slow, shaking breaths. "Mike, I-I found a bag that was already open… It looks like someone went through it in a hurry…" She sounded ready to flee, to be anywhere but baggage claim. "It's really old, like maybe from the '80s. A lot of the clothes are ripped up, and… This is so weird…" Her voice trailed away in thought.

"Laura?"

"Sorry… It's a little dizzying. I feel like I'm at a landfill."

"Well, be careful. Maybe you wandered into storage somewhere?"

"No…! Or at least I don't think I did." Her breath caught short. *"Mike–"*

"Did you find somebody?"

Shaking whispers responded, *"I-I think I found empty bullet casings."*

"As in, they've been… shot?"

"I think so! They're all wedged between the suitcases!"

The dread inching its way into his veins wasn't appreciated.

Laura continued but struggled to keep her voice low. "I-I think someone went through this to find their gun! Why would they need to do that? *What were they shooting at?*"

"Is there blood on the floor?" Mike couldn't believe he'd asked such a question to his hysterical wife.

Further panic sank its claws into her whispers. *"I can't tell! There are so many suitcases! You can hardly walk!"* Thunder shattered over Laura's head. Keeping her voice low turned into an afterthought. "The wind is rattling the front doors! I-I haven't seen a single car drive by this entire time!" Whispering and on the verge of tears, Laura confided, "Mike… I-I don't want to be here… I don't even know where *here* is anymore!"

"I'll find a way to get to you, ok? I just need time to think!"

The world was making less sense by the minute. By every shred of logic, the situation Laura found herself in should have been impossible. Assuming she was telling the truth, Mike couldn't comprehend any logical answers.

A blood-curdling scream came through the phone. Mike heard his wife stumble and suitcases wheeze under her weight. "*AHHH!*"

The phone creaked in his grip as if his fingers might shatter the plastic against his face. "Laura? *Laura, what is it?*"

"*I saw something! Something moved across the window of the VIP lounge!*"

Mike glanced toward the ceiling. An exclusive second floor boasted a relaxing getaway for the airport's premium members, separate from the coach and economy flyers of the world. A row of fogged windows was the only view available into the realm of the upper class. He could see several human-shaped silhouettes standing against the blurry glass.

Mike suggested, "Maybe it's someone who can help?"

He had never heard Laura so terrified. "T-T-That shadow wasn't shaped like any person I've ever seen…"

The sound of scrambling and frantic breath soon followed. Mike could hear her panting, as he felt like he was listening to a horror movie on his phone. "What are you doing?"

Her voice pulled thin and sharp. "*I have to get out of here, Mike! I have to get out of this airport!*"

Banging fists fell upon tempered glass to echo down the empty halls. She was beating on the doors to the exit like a crazed animal.

"The doors won't open! I can't even see the other side of the road, Mike! I can't see what's out there! Everything is covered in fog!"

"Laura! Laura, take a breath! We'll figure this out!"

"HOW? We can't even–"

Something erupted through the phone. A horrible, mind-numbing roar drowned Laura, like a gnat in a storm. He thought his device might have been broken to produce such a gut-wrenching sound. Such vibrations couldn't have been of earthly reality.

"Laura…?"

She didn't respond. Listening close, he could hear her running. Her shoes echoed off the tiled floors and empty halls of the airport. She was in a dead sprint.

The roar came again, rumbling in the background. A horrified scream merged with Laura's gasping breaths.

"Laura? *Laura!*"

Fear born of primal instinct fogged her breath through the phone. Mike had to focus to make out her shaking voice. *"There's… There's something… in here…!"*

"What–"

Squeaks parted her words from trying to talk so softly. *"I don't know! I don't know, Mike! I'm hiding behind a counter in the food court! T-There's dried blood all over the floor! I think–"*

Another guttural otherworldly scream made Mike's bones want to jump from his body. It sounded closer than before. Laura wheezed through a hand clamped over her mouth and nose to silence her breathing.

"Mike! It's going to find me! Don't let it find me!"

"Call 911! Maybe they can track your phone and–"

"No! No! What if I can't get a hold of you again? My call barely went through! I don't want to be left alone here! Please don't leave me here!"

The scream reeked of pain and all-consuming horror. Mike's mind couldn't begin to comprehend what beast could produce such a sound.

"I-It's looking for me!"

"Don't make any noise! Stay where you are! I'm going to–"

A familiar voice stole his attention. "Mike! There you are! Finally!"

Mike looked up and realized sweat was pouring down his face. Laura was weaving her way toward him through the crowd of people with her suitcase in tow.

His mind short-circuited. Nothing over the past thirty minutes would lead him to believe she should be standing in front of him. It was her face, yet he wasn't sure he would have recognized her if she hadn't called his name.

"L…Laura?" he asked, lowering his phone.

A voice came from the device. *"Mike? MIKE?"*

Laura glared at him. "I thought you would meet me at security!"

She embraced him as she always did, though something felt off. Mike couldn't place the source of uncanny dread. The simplest explanation was to believe this truly was his wife wrapping her arms around him.

"I-I… Uh…"

"Ohhh, are those for me?" Laura took the flowers from his frozen grasp and inhaled. *"They're wonderful."*

A bellow shook his phone's speakers, unnoticed.

"MIKE!" Laura's voice shrieked from beside his hip, barely audible among the crowd.

Laura stepped back. "Oh! I can't wait to tell you about the baby shower! Come on, I already got my bag." She took Mike's hand. "To home, Jeeves!"

"MIKE! MIKE! ARE YOU STILL THERE?"

"PLEASE! FOR THE LOVE OF GOD! DON'T LEAVE ME! I DON'T WANT TO BE ALONE! IT'S GOING TO–"

–click

About *Gate C12*

There's something unsettling about empty places that are meant to be bustling. They're not meant to be abandoned, and when you happen across them in such a state, you feel like you're seeing something not meant to be seen. Usually, people refer to these types of settings as 'liminal spaces'.

Gate C12 *was set in the Seattle, Washington airport, but it was based on similar experiences at the Boise, Idaho airport I frequent. It's much smaller, and thus far more prone to being deserted if you happen to arrive late at night. Shops will be closed. Security will be absent. Your feet echo down the empty halls. You might be walking with a plane's worth of other passengers, but something still isn't quite right about all those other empty terminals. It's just not normal.*

Just
Relax

TWO dexterous hands and a bottle of massage oil… It was all I could think about. After the last two days, they were a perfect recipe to relieve the stress and strain of my work trip. An eight-hour car ride, followed by a day of sitting in an uncomfortable convention center chair, had worn on my body.

Heavenly Massage and Spa, the sign read. Its glow stood out against the twilight sky like a beacon of relief. I already had the rest of the night planned out after this. It involved a pizza with double meat, and sitting in my hotel room watching TV. All I wanted was to relax before driving home tomorrow.

The tension in my shoulders burned as I walked through the door, as if it were trying to prolong its existence. My pain protested, knowing why I was there, and it knew it wouldn't be leaving the massage parlor. This was where stress came to die.

A woman behind a desk greeted me with a smile as warm as the spiced fragrance in the air. "Hello…! Can I help you?"

"I had an eight-thirty?"

Her fingers clacked across a keyboard. "Phil?"

"That's me."

"Wonderful. We have a room all ready for you. If you'll take a seat, your therapist will be out in a moment."

"Thank you."

I wasn't trying to be so curt. A mixture of mental exhaustion, tiredness, and sore muscles had taken their toll on my desire for conversation. I turned away after leaving the receptionist with a smile, hoping I hadn't been too rude. Tired clients were nothing new to them, I was sure.

A small meditation fountain bubbled next to the couch. I could have fallen asleep then and there if I wanted, but I had to wait. Just a few more minutes and I could let myself melt away from the world for an hour.

"Phil?"

I looked up. A woman was standing in an open doorway leading to a dimly lit hall lined with rooms. She was a young, attractive, Asian woman, likely in her early thirties. Her petite stature made me question if she had the weight for the deep-tissue care I was after, but considering I made the appointment only two hours prior, I was happy just to be here.

Standing, I approached the smiling woman and noticed I had nearly two feet over her in height. I am a taller man, but this was also a very short woman.

"My name is Mari; I'll be your massage therapist tonight." She motioned down the hall. "We'll be in the last door on the left."

I led the way, trying to keep as quiet as possible when passing the other massage rooms. If it were me, I wouldn't want loud footsteps interrupting my session.

Our room greeted me with candles and a track of meditation music playing over hidden speakers. The massage table looked more comfortable than my hotel bed. I couldn't wait.

Mari closed the door behind us. "So what are we working on today?"

I instinctively rubbed my neck. "All upper body, mostly neck and shoulders."

"I can certainly do that. Any extras? Hot stones? Essential oils?"

I was tempted to say yes to everything and bury myself under the ultimate blanket of relaxation, but I had to maintain some level of self-control. "No, thank you," I ultimately declined.

"Not a problem!" She cracked the door to step out. "Go ahead and dress down to your comfort level and lay on your stomach. I'll be back in a few minutes."

"Sounds good."

The door closed leaving me to undress. There was no hesitation as I stripped naked. It was a strange intimacy, but I would never be able to relax if my boxers were strangling my legs. Not to mention the heated bed was like a lover's embrace when I climbed under the sheets.

I waited, staring at the floor through the headrest. My only hope was that I didn't start to snore halfway through the session.

A gentle tap came from the door.

"Come in," I called.

She entered unseen. I listened to her moving about the room preparing various supplies and setting the lights lower. The design on the carpet blurred in the dimness. I wasn't able to see her, but I could feel her standing at my side. The air was warm when she folded the sheet away from my back and tucked it around my hips.

"I'm glad you could fit me in on such short notice…" I mumbled. "I would hate to drive home with my neck like this."

"You called at just the right time! My original

appointment fell through." She pressed her fingers down my back, as if searching for the areas most in need. "Are you from out of town?"

My eyes drifted closed as she started to work. "I'm here for a business conference... Busy, but boring as hell. Barely managed to sneak away for– *Ngh!*"

Her strength took me by surprise. A knot over my shoulder blade screamed under her thumb.

"How's that pressure?"

"*Perfect...*"

Mari worked deeper across my shoulders, kneading and rolling over my stress. Her efforts made me wince. I had asked for deep-tissue work, but I wasn't expecting to feel it in my bones. It was excruciatingly wonderful, and I felt several out-of-place ribs move under her hands. Mari was stronger than she looked. I thought I could hear my joints popping from her work.

"That's... perfect..." I told her again.

She laughed softly. "Your coworkers weren't envious of your massage?"

"They... don't know I came here..." I wasn't sure my voice was even comprehensible at this point. My energy level was low enough that my words might have been a series of garbles. "Can you get my lower back a little mo– *Ow!*"

Something pricked my shoulder when she touched me. I jolted at the sharp sensation before settling once more under her hands.

"Sorry!" Mari giggled, looming over me. "I have a bit of an electric personality..."

As much as I understood, the shock had set me back. I shifted on the table, trying to find peace once more. The spot on my shoulder burned like a bee sting and throbbed under her fingers.

"Can we... avoid that shoulder for a few minutes?"

Mari paid my request no mind. "Just relax... Let me melt that stress away..."

As jolting as the shock had been, I could feel rest returning. Mari's hands were miracle workers. The spot on my shoulder dulled to a light tingling.

"*Pressure still good...?*" her voice drifted from far away like an attentive lover.

"Mhm..."

This woman knew what she was doing. No part of my back was left unattended. She moved slow and firm over my muscles, and yet her hands must have been flying to cover so much ground in so little time. I melted, becoming putty in her fingers.

My eyes drifted closed. I have nearly an hour of this heavenly torture left to enjoy? Life was too good. I didn't deserve such delight. I might have to come to this conference again next year just to get another massage.

"*Now breathe in deep...*"

My nose whistled when I inhaled, feeling her hands press against my rising back.

"*And out...*"

I released, only for my breath to catch in my throat. My eyes opened at a strange sensation. Something didn't feel right. Was there a third hand on my back?

Confusion made my drifting mind do several flips. There couldn't have been another hand massaging me, and yet, the presence was undeniable. I cast my eyes about the floor in search of another person's shadow. There was none, as well as no auditory hint of someone else in the room.

We were alone, yet I could count six arms between the two of us. Twenty fingers running over my back.

"Everything alright...?" Mari inquired softly. Two hands sank themselves into my shoulders while another pair worked their way down my spine.

"I... Uh..."

A fifth pressed itself against my lower back. The sensation was uncanny. Mari's hands were everywhere, caressing my back and arms with rising intensity. Something wasn't right. Had I fallen asleep and slipped into some kind of nightmare?

My curiosity was too great. I tried to move and lift my head enough for a peek at my surroundings, but firm pressure held me against the table.

"Stay down please... It's company policy." Mari's voice dripped like a salivating predator. It had grown deeper.

Sweat peppered my skin, mixing with the lotion. Although my heart was racing, my body was heavier than lead. I was numb, paralyzed, and unable to move under her skilled fingers. An ocean had swallowed my mind into a gaping abyss.

It became more difficult to keep my eyes focused. The carpet grew blurry and swirled beneath me. A misshapen shadow moved into my field of vision. Weary, I saw Mari's feet as she stood over me rubbing my neck. Feeling an additional set of hands on my thighs at the same time, was less than comforting.

Her breath was hot and humid. It washed over my skin in thick blankets. As tired and leaden as I was, Mari appeared invigorated. Enthralled. Almost... eager.

"Are you feeling relaxed...?"

Her voice was changing. No longer was it a sweet, inviting tone. Slime and lust coated her words when they oozed from her mouth. Between her rasps, were strange stretching noises like muscle and sinew pulling apart. Her words were far away, as if she stood across the room. Clacking bones and joints rattled together with muffled collisions. My mind could only equate it to someone kneading a bag of skinned animal remains.

I didn't dare answer her insidious question. I don't think I could have even if I found the courage. My body refused to move. As deep as she penetrated my muscles, the dozens of hands were now only a dull presence on my body.

Something dripped on my back. It spread over my skin and ran across the nape of my neck. It couldn't have been massage oil. It was too thick. Too viscous. It reeked of rancidity, and stung wherever it touched.

"You need to relax…"

How deeply I wished that I could. I tried to struggle but nothing happened. My back felt like flames were leaping from my pores. It felt like her fingers were trying to tear me apart. I didn't remember her nails being that sharp at the start. The sheets were wet beneath me, from what, I didn't dare to guess.

The room sounded as if it were slithering. I knew it couldn't have been, but the sounds were *everywhere.* Unexplainable shadows passed in and out of my tiny view. No longer could I hear the soothing meditation drifting from the speakers; the atmosphere was permeated by Mari's breathing and that sickening sound of pulling flesh. I'd lost count of the number of hands upon my form.

"Let's have you flip over…"

I wasn't being offered a choice. With my body as limp as a doll's, I was cradled in a blanket of limbs and hands. They wrapped around me to spin the room, bringing my vision toward the ceiling. I wish the lights had been off.

A monstrous thing loomed over me in the grim dimness of flickering candlelight. Mari was gone, her torso having stretched and pulled into an elongated horror multiple times its original length. Her serpentine body dominated the room and coiled around the bed. Dozens of arms sprawled from the wriggling pillar of pale bulging skin. Her nakedness was not of fantasy but that of sheer nightmare, as I was held captive by this mass of centipede flesh. Her grinning head stood at the top, while she hunched against the ceiling. Black hair fell over her shoulders in oily spiderwebs. The putrid saliva running from her teeth to her neck made me wish I could gag as it trickled between her sagging breasts.

"Feeling relaxed…?"

I wanted nothing more than to scream as I heard that terrible mouth speak. My eyes couldn't even widen out of fear. Control was gone. I was a prisoner in my own skin as her arms tightened their coil. I stared ahead like a lifeless doll. A spirit trapped in a paralyzed husk.

A grin spread across her face, far wider than what should have been possible. *"Good…"*

The last of the candlelight dimmed behind her shifting form. I could only watch as her cheeks split from mouth to ear. Her jaw opened, stretching ever wider until a bloody gash opened down the center of her chin. A chasm split her mandible before splaying the front of her gullet down to her collarbones. Her visage unfolded, blossoming into a seething flower of voracious hunger leading into a serpentine body. I wanted to scream at that unhinged jaw of seething teeth and darkness as it fell upon me, but I couldn't. Even when I felt her slick insides meet against my body, and those nightmarish teeth sank into my legs, my body refused to protest.

I was just too relaxed.

<u>About *Just Relax*</u>

It shouldn't come as a surprise that this idea came to me during a massage. I was looking for my next story idea while lying there with my mind wandering in and out of a half-sleep, and wouldn't you know it, I found a way to make a massage terror-inducing.

Take it from me; when you're naked on a table and can't see what's going on around you, the last thing you want is to start wondering what the masseuse is really doing.

Makes Your Skin Crawl

THERE is a building I pass every day on a walk during my lunch break. It's not exactly unique. In fact, it's extraordinarily mundane. The structure is plain concrete and three stories tall. I would say it's windowless, but that's not entirely correct. Thin rectangular cut-outs line the sides, though their glass is fogged brown, as if the interior is filled with rusty smog. It's eerily reminiscent of the abandoned-looking train depots you find along the tracks in the countryside where you never see anyone working. Even the front door– the only door, I might add– is a dull black-painted metal.

In short, it's a building you wouldn't acknowledge unless you were looking for it. Even I only noticed it after walking by for nearly a year. But since then, I haven't been able to stop wondering as to its purpose. I've never had the courage to venture inside, much less a reason aside from my curiosity. There were no house numbers, no business name, no sign, no marketing of any kind. It was devoid of any identification.

The area around it was clean and well-manicured with a fair amount of grass, trees, and even a small footpath. Based on the trees' height, the building has been standing for well over one hundred years. These are the kind of trees you see on Main Street that have been around since the city's conception. Some days, it feels like the building is trying to hide amongst the clean-cut landscaping, like it's all a distraction. But perhaps the weirdest thing about this building… *is the lack of people.*

There is no employee parking lot, no reserved spots along the road. Oh, I've seen people go inside, *but that's it.* In all my years of walking by, not once have I seen anyone exit through that single front door. I know it's not entirely impossible for me to not have encountered someone leaving. After all, there's always a chance. But when I've seen dozens enter, I would have expected to see *at least one person exit.*

My coworkers at the office look at me like I'm crazy when I bring it up. You might have thought I inquired about a medieval castle down the street. In reality, I'm sure it's not anything out of the ordinary. It's probably some kind of government building or maybe an exclusive underground nightclub. Likely something someone like me isn't on the up-and-up enough to know about.

Internet searches reveal nothing, which isn't surprising; I had no address to go off of, only the location. Online satellite maps showed nothing aside from an empty park. I thought maybe they weren't up to date enough to include the building, however, they showed my house, which was built only two years ago. Not to mention this building doesn't even look like it's from this century. A visit to city hall could prove useful if they have any records, but I didn't care *that* much to put myself through such torture.

In truth, I enjoyed the hint of the unknown. Walking past this strange unmarked building brought a dose of mystery to an otherwise normal work day. Putting too much effort into revealing, what was certainly, a mundane reality wasn't worth killing the mystique.

That is… Until my wife got the invitation.

I walked through the door of our home to find her pouring over a letter. It was delicate and ornate with gold-pressed lettering that I could see from across the room.

"What's that? Someone getting married?" I asked.

Claire jumped from her chair. I had hardly ever seen her so excited. Her hands shook as she approached with the letter in hand. "Howard! *Look, Howard!*" She shoved it into my face. *"It's from the Secta Group!"*

Having the logo fill my field of vision didn't answer my question. "Never heard of them…"

I took the paper. It was fancy. Running my fingers over the pressed lettering was oddly satisfying. However, there wasn't much info to be found.

> Claire Holmes, you have been selected.
> Welcome to the Secta Group.
> Please arrive promptly at 6 p.m. on September
> the 5th.
> Invitation only.

I glanced between Claire and her precious letter several times. Her eyes were like full moons as she stood trembling with excitement.

Still not understanding, I scratched my head. "What's it for…?"

The neighbors probably heard her gasp in horror. *"THE SECTA GROUP, HOWARD!"*

"Right, but what is the invitation *for?* Did you enter a

contest?"

Claire laughed as if I were a child inquiring about Santa Claus. "If you don't know, you don't know." She snatched the paper away and buried her face into its folds. A moan came from her as she closed her eyes and swooned. "*Mmmm...* Doesn't it smell *amazing?*"

I was blinded by white when she shoved it under my nose. I inhaled with little payoff. "Doesn't smell like much to me."

Claire only continued to swoon and inhale, almost dancing with the letter. In the meantime, I decided to investigate this organization. My heart danced in my chest when the first Google result showed a picture of my mysterious building.

"*This is it!*" I burst out, jabbing my finger at my phone.

"Mmm, what is?"

"It's the building! The weird unmarked building I pass on my walk every day? Remember?"

Her eyes sparkled while reading the paper once again. "Of course it is!"

I stared. "You knew?"

"Oh, Howard... It's the Secta Group..." Claire approached and patted my shoulder with a dreamy grin. "If you don't know, you don't know." Her lungs filled to the brim when she inhaled the letter's essence once more, culminating in an eye-fluttering sigh. "Ooooh, I can't wait."

"Wait, *you're going?*"

"I *have* to go! How can I not? It's the *Secta Group, Howard. The Secta Group!*"

I don't think I'd seen so much excitement oozing from

her pores since our wedding day. "This says it's for tomorrow… Weren't you going to your sister's baby shower after work? Shouldn't you–"

Her mood changed as my protest continued. Defensiveness swam in her voice. "Howard, I *will* go. You can't stop me. Do you hear me? *If you try to stop me, you WILL regret it! I swear I will lea–*"

"You can go, you can go!" I raised my hands in defeat. The sudden 180 in her demeanor had caught me off guard. It didn't feel like I was talking to my wife. Trying to diffuse the situation, I asked, "Think I can come too?"

"Did you get an invitation?"

"No…"

Claire shrugged and pointed to her letter. "Says right here: *invitation only.*"

*   *   *

NONE of my coworkers recognized the Secta Group when I asked them the next day. Given Claire's excitement, I thought for sure I was simply out of the loop. I even had some of them text their partners about it. No one had ever heard of them.

To say I was nervous was an understatement. How trustworthy could an organization be if it had no online presence and was utterly unheard of? Was this some kind of scam? I still couldn't believe Claire had thrown her sister's baby shower away so easily, but given her venom-spitting reaction when I suggested she not go, I was hesitant to say anything more. I arrived home early just in case, so I could make sure I saw her off.

Boiling excitement refused to let Claire sit still. From the moment I came home from work, she remained sitting at our kitchen table staring at the letter longingly. It had her completely transfixed. There was no tearing her away, not even when her sister called wondering where she was.

Her time of departure arrived despite my apprehensions. Looking at the clock, like a child in grade school excited for the start of Christmas break, she rose to embark. There was no farewell when she opened the door.

"Wait! Want me to drive you?" I offered.

"Nope!" Her reply came fast and sharp without a moment's thought.

"I was thinking maybe we can grab dinner downtown after you're done or something? Hit a Friday happy hour? There's a new place opening up that–"

"*I said no, Howard! Drop it.*"

There was a snarl on her lips but brilliant excitement in her eyes. I was keeping her from her destination. It felt like I'd just been snapped at by a dog when I tried to take its precious bone.

"Ok… Let me know when you're on your way home."

She left without another word. No goodbye. No assurance of her love for me. The apocalypse couldn't have kept her from the Secta Group.

It was dark by the time Claire returned. Her car pulled into the garage with an emotionless hum. I tried listening to the slam of her car door to pick up on any form of sourness but it was strangely soft. She stumbled through the door moments later.

I tried to match her original energy. The excitement bubbling inside me, enough to make me shake, wasn't a lie. "Well? How was it?"

"Fine…"

Her purse fell to the floor. She barely gave me a look. There was a dire sluggishness in her movements. She moved as if she hadn't slept in a week and was given someone else's legs to walk home with. A dead gaze stared at the floor in front of her as she made her way through the kitchen toward the stairs.

"It's pretty late; do you want some dinner?"

Claire turned to look at me. I thought she might fall over from the way she was swaying. "No…"

Her voice was rough and distant. In the few hours she'd been gone, her face had aged a decade. The skin seemed to sag from her cheekbones and her eyes were sunken. If I were to walk past this person on the street, I wouldn't think it was my wife.

"Claire? Are you feeling alright?"

"I'm just tired…"

"What happened? How did it go? With the Secta Group?"

Her cold eyes stared at me for a time. "Secta Group…?"

My brain didn't know how to respond at this point. It was doing somersaults trying to decode my wife's erratic behavior. The idea of an affair came to mind but even that sounded too far-fetched given her state. "The Secta Group? The invitation you received for today?" My voice was starting to rise in volume and waver with emotion. "Where did you go? You were so excited!"

"I don't know what you're talking about…"

She turned her back and started climbing the stairs with

strenuous effort. There was no denial in her voice. The bluntness of her reply might as well have been a bat to the chest.

"Claire… I'm only trying to–"

"I'm tired… I'm going to bed…"

Her slumping form vanished upstairs into the darkness. The grate of her voice still scratched in my ears. Overhead, I heard the bed creak with her weight. The couch did the same when I collapsed in deep, worry-filled thought. In over fifteen years of marriage, never had I seen my wife go to bed without washing her face.

*　　*　　*

MY concern didn't vanish after a night's sleep. I had hoped Claire was simply exhausted after her mysterious meeting, but her mannerisms remained odd on Saturday.

The smell was the first thing to strike me when I woke up. A strange scent like rotting wood permeated our sheets and stung my nostrils. Claire was already up. Her side of the bed had been sloppily made; a far cry from the military-like precision she usually employs.

Our garden was empty of her presence when I peeked out of the bedroom window. Most Saturdays, I would awake to find her tending the flowers or weeding. Instead, I saw her shadow shuffling down the hall. Anxiety gripped my chest when she wandered into our room. Her attention barely paid me any notice while I got dressed. Her hair was brushed but looked as though a toddler had assumed the responsibility and her t-shirt was on backward.

"Morning, hon!" I greeted, attempting to skirt a possible bad mood.

"Good morning…"

The response was dull and grating. She didn't bother to look at me, only drifting into our bathroom before exiting moments later and returning to the hall.

"Claire?"

"Hm?"

I realized I was frightened to speak to her. The change in her demeanor was off putting, but there was something else. Something primal that was sparking every human instinct rooted inside my brain telling my feet to run.

Maybe it was that mildewy smell following her like a ghost…

Against my trepidation, I asked, "Do you feel like going to the farmer's market this morning?"

Claire's words sounded drowned in syrup while descending the stairs. "You go… I have things to do."

"We could get lunch and–"

"No…" her rejection drifted from downstairs. "Too much to do…"

I watched her. I stayed home all day, making myself look busy while keeping within range of my wife.

Believe me when I tell you, *she didn't do a damn thing.*

Most of her day was spent wandering from room to room. At first I thought she might have been looking for something, but then I noticed there was little rhyme or reason to her movements. It was as if she were in a constant state of going somewhere only to forget why. Sometimes she would pause, standing still to stare at a wall before becoming enamored with her nails. I could hear her clicking and picking at them even in the next room.

I'll admit I was frightened to approach her. Claire was disheveled and haggard. Strands of hair hung over her face like a veil concealing the sanity of the woman I loved.

I wondered if I ought to take her to the doctor. So far as I knew, she wasn't showing any signs of a stroke. She was coherent, just... not herself. I vacuumed several times during the day, if only to wipe away the trails she'd made in the carpet from her dragging feet. Looking at them was causing more anxiety than I care to admit.

By the time we ate dinner, our entire house smelled like our sheets. Moldy... Wet... Damp... Like soaked towels left on the floor for a week.

"Claire?" I called from the kitchen. A pot of spaghetti sat in front of me. The steam was oddly cleansing. As lovingly as possible, I said, "Come eat dinner, hon!"

The sound of her stumbling down the stairs toward me... Every little *thump... thump... thump...* sounded like the steps of someone using another person's legs. It made my hair stand on end.

She fell into a chair at our table and waited with a slight hunch in her back. There was no physical reaction when I placed a bowl of noodles in front of her.

"Thank you..."

I sat opposite. For the first time that day, I was forced to look her in the eyes, and my body wanted to run. Her brown gaze stared at me from behind a curtain of messed hair. I wish I could say they were full of sadness, or despair, or anger.

Anything that might explain her behavior. But I felt no such emotion. There was only a cold, calculating stare. As if she were a predator without an appetite examining a future meal.

She placed her hands on the table and began eating. The spaghetti came up in droves on her fork before entering her mouth. It gnashed and spewed sauce in every direction. Her lips moved with disconnected flapping motions. Watching her eat made me nauseous, I'm ashamed to say.

"Hon…" I reached a hand across the table to grasp hers. My own food sat untouched, my appetite nonexistent. "Is everything alright? You–"

"*Grhn!*"

She grunted and pulled her hand away. Something flashed in her eyes when she looked up from her meal. A warning.

My own hand recoiled with hers, though not before trying to maintain my grip. There was a sensation as my fingers tightened around her palm. A sense of looseness. It was subtle at first but became grotesquely pronounced when she pulled away. Folds of skin bunched against my grip and wrinkled down her fingers. It felt like I might have pulled off an ill-fitting glove had I held any tighter.

"Clai–"

I was looking harder at her now, scanning her body. Her face was sunken and melted like wax. Her elbow dragged across the table as her hand worked to transport pasta. Around her neck, was a pile of wrinkles belonging to someone twice her age. Marinara sauce ran down her chin to settle in the crevices around her collarbones.

The longer I stared, the worse it became. Horror begged me to flee as I realized my wife's skin didn't fit.

*　　　*　　　*

I didn't eat that night. I couldn't. Not after watching Claire. The pit in my stomach was more than enough to sustain me.

She'd gone upstairs after finishing her dinner. I could hear her moving around for the next few hours like a lost zombie. It wasn't until around ten, when finally, the noises stopped. She was asleep.

I was left wondering what to do. Something was wrong with my wife. Anxiety gnawed at my gut, but my eyes were heavy. Did I want to sleep next to her? Of course I knew I *should*, but could I stand to do it? Clearly she was going through something. Regardless of her appearance and strange behavior, what kind of husband would I be if I abandoned her in a time of need?

Climbing the stairs was harder than I care to admit. As I neared our room, I could hear her breathing. It was fast and short. Unnatural for someone supposed to be asleep. A part of me wished I could spend all night brushing my teeth.

Against every fiber of my being, I slid into bed next to her under the cover of darkness. I wanted to be quick before my eyes had time to adjust and catch sight of her. Maybe she was simply tired. Maybe *I* was tired and was just seeing things that weren't there. It's difficult to believe she could change so dramatically overnight.

But I didn't know what went on at the Secta Group. In that mystery building that haunted my lunch walks. That fact ran through my mind countless times as I lay there listening to her erratic breathing. It might not be so bad if our bed didn't smell like mold.

*   *   *

IT was still dark when I opened my eyes. Claire was shifting in her sleep. In the dim grayness, I saw her roll onto her side and face away from me. She almost looked normal from this angle, like her old self.

But there was something off with her hair. There was a strange part going down the back of her head, as if a surgeon had needed to open her skull down the middle and the hair hadn't grown back. I couldn't place what looked so odd about it until my eyes fully came to. It wasn't a part…

It was a zipper.

The metallic seam ran right down the back of her head. With how messy her hair had been, it's no wonder I hadn't noticed it sooner. But now, even in the dead of night, it was plain as day. The black teeth reflected the neighbor's porch light through the window. I didn't want to believe it was really there, but it stared back, going down her cranium and neck. A slight lift of the sheets revealed it traveling all the way down her back before ending at her lumbar.

I could tell her skin was loose around it, like the metal was pulling at the slack. There was a pull tab near the top of her head. I knew I should leave it alone, but my hand was moving before I could decide otherwise.

The puller was cold between my thumb and finger. Barely any force was used to grasp it. Don't ask me how I expected to unzip my wife's body without waking her. Nothing about this felt right.

It sounded like an old leather jacket when I pulled.

Slowly at first, but noticing no reaction, I decided to finish what I'd started. I unzipped her down to her mid back in one slow motion. The sound cut through the night like a scream, but when I was done, nothing. Her breathing had stopped; I couldn't see the side of her torso rising any longer. The back of her body was splayed open like an old handbag. I don't know what I expected to see. It certainly wasn't soul-crushing darkness, though.

There was nothing. Nothing but inky black inside of her. The sight completely absorbed me. It made the surrounding room look illuminated with sunlight by comparison. Slowly, I extended a hand to reach inside. Surely it couldn't be empty. There had to be some sense to this.

My fingers were mere inches away before I froze. Claire's body had started to undulate and throb, as if something were moving inside of her. The zipper's opening flared wider. Within, the darkness bristled.

It started pouring out of her in a thick mass. Stunned, I didn't have a chance to back away. I was surprised when it collided with me and it wasn't wet. It moved like a fluid but felt more solid.

The dim light started to play over it. Thousands of tiny, needle-like legs revealed themselves. They all wiggled from the black mass to claw over each other and right themselves.

Pitch-black cockroaches.

Midnight centipedes.

Black widows.

They flooded our sheets. There seemed no end to them as I saw Claire's figure deflate. Her body caved in on itself as her contents rushed out.

They were everywhere. My body instinctively flailed,

throwing the sheets off and swatting my hands over my front. At my side, Claire was no more than the limp naked suit of a woman. I wanted to scream, but the scurrying horrors only took the opportunity to fill my mouth.

*   *   *

SWEAT soaked through the sheets when I jolted upright in bed. My chest was pounding. I could still feel the spiders tickling my throat as I gasped for air and looked around in a panic.

It was still our room, but spider-free. The clock read 2:05 am. Claire was just as I'd left her when I climbed into bed. Cautious, I poked her shoulder.

She rolled over without a sound. No sign of a zipper. No strange part in her hair. No flood of black widows and cockroaches. Just a dream.

I laid back trying to catch my breath. This was becoming too much. Whatever that Secta Group had done with Claire, I couldn't even sleep soundly next to her now. The ceiling loomed over me as I pondered. It had all started with that building. The answers were there. Could I really live like this? Could I go to work on Monday and walk by that gray building and not go mad wondering what had gone on inside those walls?

The answer was, a very obvious, *no*.

Streetlights were flying by before I knew it. There would certainly not be any more sleep for me tonight. Claire probably wouldn't even notice I had left. I needed to know what happened. I needed some form of clarity. Had something really happened to Claire, or was I the one going insane? Had that building really wormed itself into my mind to such a degree that

I was dreaming about unzipping my wife's skin? My knuckles turned white around the steering wheel as I wondered.

The roads were deserted. It was oddly cold being so alone on the highway, even with the heater on. I tried thinking about how best to navigate to the building, but couldn't form the mental path. Where should I park? What were the crossroads? Any landmarks? My mind drew only blanks. The picture of the building in my head was barely maintained. Why the hell was it so difficult to envision?

I drove around the downtown area for two hours searching for the property. In the darkness, nothing looked familiar. I couldn't get my bearings. After a while, I started wondering if I was truly going mad. I must have driven up and down every street looking for the thing.

Finally, as the first rays of the sun were coming over the horizon, I decided to park at my office. Maybe I couldn't manage to drive to the building, but I *knew* I could walk to it. I walked to it every day. My feet knew the way even if my brain didn't.

Within ten minutes I was there. The scene was so familiar. I must have driven by the building ten times. How I failed to see it only further frustrated me.

As always, there were no signs of life aside from a dull rusty illumination coming through the windows. Stepping onto the property for the first time felt wrong. Like I wasn't meant to be there. Like I wasn't even supposed to know it existed. I noticed my skin breaking out in goosebumps the closer I approached the front door. Who knew gray concrete could be so uninviting.

The metal boomed when I pounded against it. Of course there was no answer; it was early dawn on a Sunday. But given everything else happening because of this place, I almost expected someone to answer. But I wasn't about to give up.

Going around, I stuck to the wall and looked for any kind of window I could see into. A muffled thunking sound, like that of a factory, vibrated the concrete wall under my hand. I was so focused on looking at eye level that it almost went unnoticed in my rush: a narrow glass pane along the ground was hidden behind a bush. It looked like a window to a basement. It was hidden well enough I never could have seen it from the sidewalk.

I fell to my hands and knees, crawling behind the greenery. Morning dew soaked through my pajamas with ease but I ignored the chill. A snake could have bitten me and I wouldn't have noticed. I only wanted to see inside. One glimpse. One piece of closure. Any kind of clue where my wife had gone.

The glass was coated in a layer of rusty brown. Wiping the surface did little to help visibility. All of the grime must have been on the inside. Still, I could see foggy shadows moving within.

It took a little bit for the shapes to form something my brain could make sense of, and even then, I wasn't sure what I was looking at.

Dark figures moved by in a blur. They looked to be several meters away from the window and moving on a track. There was a diagonal sway to them, as if they were suspended. They almost looked like meaty wetsuits traveling along a dry cleaner's conveyor belt. The longer I watched, the sharper the whir of them flying down the metal rail grew.

There was more movement further down, but nothing I could understand. It was clearly conscious motion, but the blurry shadow couldn't have belonged to a person; it was too elongated and hunched forward.

Frustration rose to a boil. This wasn't helping. I had no more idea about what the Secta Group was or why my wife was so different. Nothing more than blurry shadows.

My hand smacking against the glass was like a firecracker in the early morning. It didn't break, but I was determined. Heart pounding, I smacked it again with more force. There was a reaction from the shadows inside. I was making myself known, but that wouldn't stop me.

The next time, I balled my hand into a fist. It was enough to crack the pane and bruise my flesh. I didn't know what would happen when I broke through. I don't even know what I planned to do. I just knew I wanted to see inside this building. My fist raised a final time. Lips flared in madness, I brought it down only for my strike to stop short.

There were lights behind me flashing red and blue. I looked over my shoulder to see a cop car pulling up to the edge of the surrounding park. They had to have been there for me. There was no one else around! But how did they know? How did they get here so fast? I had only found the basement window a minute ago!

Their doors opened. Two officers stepped out, only to stand motionless with their eyes trained on me. Maybe it was their opaque sunglasses, maybe it was the way their skin didn't sit right on their skeletons, but I ran as fast as I could. The building's grassy property had never seemed so big as I fled. Among the buildings downtown, I felt safer, far away from their gaze.

I had to duck into an alley to catch my breath. I don't know why they made no effort to chase me. Likely they only wanted to scare me off the property. *But why?*

The crushing weight of helpless mystery bore down on me. I doubled over and held my head in my hands. Was I simply going crazy? Surely this wasn't all in my mind. *What is the damn Secta Group?*

A shrill tone brought me back to earth. My phone was ringing. I don't know why I was so surprised to see Claire's photo as the ID.

"Where are you…?" her voice came through, deadpan as ever.

"I–" I took a moment to catch my breath and compose myself. "I had to run into the office real quick. I'll be home soon!"

Claire sounded as uninterested as ever. "Ok."

"I-I love you."

Click

*   *   *

THE house was quiet when I walked through the door, even for early on a Sunday morning. Claire was standing at the kitchen sink staring out the window with a blank expression. She looked a little better than she did at dinner last night. It was impossible to know how long the faucet had been running.

"Sorry," I started, "something came up at work and–"

She interrupted, "Someone dropped that off for you." Claire turned. There was a slight grin on her otherwise emotionless face. The first hint of a smile I had seen in two days. The rest of her face refused to emote and left me with uncanny chills.

I blinked, feeling perplexed before noticing an envelope on our counter. It was so white it almost glowed.

There was nothing written on it, no sender or recipient. It didn't need one. I knew who, or what, it had come from.

The world slowed around me. Already, I had witnessed what the contents of this letter had done to Claire. Would I have gotten my letter regardless? Or was I close to something… Something the Secta Group didn't want anyone knowing, and they wanted me out of the picture?

Claire was staring directly at me. Unwavering, unblinking, with that toothy deadpan smile plastered on her sagging face.

"Aren't you going to open it, Howard?"

She almost sounded like her old self. Her tone was full of encouragement, like a ghoul daring someone to take a step closer. I swallowed, extending a hand. This could be my chance to see inside that building. To get my answers. They knew I was getting close! They knew I had almost gotten in! Maybe I could resist the letter's effects… I could take the invitation… withstand their seduction… use it to get inside and *finally see what's in that damn building.*

The envelope was stiff in my fingers under Claire's watchful gaze. I could resist it. I had to. I knew what was waiting for me within the seal. I would be mentally prepared, able to fight back and fake my way into the Secta Group.

Steeled against what was to come, I broke the seal and breathed in deep.

That scent…

Oh what a wonderful scent.

A delightful fragrance sent my heart pounding. Within was a letter… *My* letter… White with gold lettering.

This was it.

My hands shook as I read. Every inhale was intoxicating and filled me with unbridled delight. Oh I could barely contain my excitement!

This was really it!

> *Howard Holmes, you have been selected.*
> *Welcome to the Secta Group.*
> *Please arrive promptly at 10 a.m. on September the 7th.*
> *Invitation only.*

The Secta Group! *The Secta Group wanted ME!*

I couldn't inhale deep enough. My lungs couldn't get enough of that aroma. Excitement was ready to erupt from my body. I read the letter again, and again, and again, taking in every word…every syllable…every curve of every letter.

God, it smelled good. It was beautiful.

Priceless.

This invitation was worth more than my soul.

Should I frame it? Show it off? Claire and I could hang ours side-by-side!

"Welcome to the Group, dear…"

It was happening. It was really happening. My lips parted, mouthing 'the Secta Group' in child-like delight.

I turned my gaze to my wife. She'd never looked so beautiful. *"It's the Secta Group, Claire!"*

I *had* to go.

About *Makes Your Skin Crawl*

This story is based on a real building.

Unfortunately, it isn't nearly as exciting as the one from this story. I used to take walks during work and would loop around a small park area before heading back. In the middle of the park is a large, gray, brick building with tiny inescapable windows and a front door I never seem to see people leave from. It also has signs designating it a historical landmark.

For those curious, it's the old Boise Assay Office building. It was built in 1871. Idaho was once ranked third in the nation for the amount of gold being mined. Prospectors would go to this building to have their ores appraised and purified. The gold rush has died down, in case you didn't know. Nowadays, the building serves as the State Historical Preservation Office and the Archaeological Survey of Idaho. Not nearly as insidious as whatever the Secta Group has going on, but you never know... They do have those tiny windows behind bushes lining the basement. Take a peek in there if you're ever in town. There probably isn't some nefarious plot hidden behind the glass. Probably...

In the Deep

WATER stretched before Amelia in an endless terrain of waves. Normally, the vast expanse would have made her uneasy, but watching from the air brought a sense of calm. The small seaplane's engine hummed over the sound of rushing wind to reach deafening levels.

Amelia craned her neck to look into the dizzying blue below. At an altitude of 1500 feet, the varying elevations of the seafloor granted dark shadows to the ocean's surface. In the afternoon, the water must have looked clear and beautiful. However, as the sun neared the horizon behind them, the ocean adopted a darkened appearance of mystery.

"Anything out there?"

Amelia jumped when a voice tinged with a ghost of an Aussie accent came through her headset. A grin parted the pilot's scraggly beard. Bronze skin and middle-aged wrinkles betrayed how long he'd lived on the African coast. A sun-worn nametag hung on a button-up read 'Hank'.

"Nothing but water!" Amelia said into her own microphone.

"Kind of fun watching how quickly the seafloor drops off, isn't it?"

The thought sent chills down Amelia's spine. She didn't need to be reminded; her overactive mind was already busy adding massive slithering shadows under the surface without the need for further commentary.

"It gets over five thousand meters deep here between the islands! That's three mi–"

"Three miles! I know…" Amelia nodded. The cheap leather of the seat squeaked under her tightening grip.

"Ah, bit afraid of the depths, eh?" Scratching his head, Hank stared ahead at the world of water. "Probably better if you don't think about it. Got a couple hundred miles to go yet! Maybe about four or five hours assuming this headwind doesn't get worse."

Amelia tried to calm herself but the cabin felt smaller with every breath. "Right…"

"So what brings ya out this far? Most of you scientist types stick to Madagascar!"

"Well, all of the surrounding islands still have a lot to offer in terms of research."

"Shit, even Merime? Thing is a spit of land compared to the others! Barely enough people to call it inhabited."

Discussing work was a welcome change from the miles of dark water churning below. Amelia was more than happy to share. "*Especially* Merime! It's the smallest islands that offer the greatest differences in evolution, fairly similar to the Galapagos. Even though it's only eighty miles or so south of Réunion, their species of birds have evolved completely different from–"

"You know, I never really understood the whole evolution deal." Hank filled his mouth with a stash of sunflower seeds. "If we came from monkeys, then why are there still monkeys?" He spit several shells out a tiny window. Amelia had to keep herself from gagging as she watched them stick to the outside and slide along the glass leaving trails of saliva. "Doesn't make a lot of sense to me!"

The scent of soggy sunflower seeds filled the cabin. Their flight couldn't be over soon enough. Amelia was suddenly wishing she hadn't taken the cheapest option. "Actually, that's a common misconception. We didn't evolve *from* monkeys; we share a common ancestor with them whose evolution branched into two separate–"

"*Crap, hang on!*"

The plane lurched after what sounded like a part of the engine blowing open. Amelia feared she might have to pay a fee for the marks her nails were leaving in Hank's seat.

The pilot threw his bag of seeds to the ground and took the wheel in both hands. "Aw shit…"

"*What was that?*" Smoke rushed from the front of the plane. Fear gripped Amelia's chest as she watched their propeller grind to a halt.

"Looks like somethin' seized up!" Hank yelled.

The plane vibrated with final death throes before its mechanics went totally silent. Sudden deceleration pulled Amelia's stomach into her throat. Hank's arms shook as he struggled to steer the plane against the headwind.

"Knew I shouldn't have used that cheap oil!"

"*Are we going to crash?*"

"No no no… We're still in a seaplane!"

Several shells flew from his lips. "We're gonna glide real gentle-like and land her in the water!"

"Can't we *glide* to Merime?"

Hank's chuckle made her shiver. "You want to glide three hundred miles with no engine and a headwind? Missy, we got maybe two miles until our toes are wet!"

"And then what? WE'RE A HUNDRED MILES FROM LAND!"

"Don't you worry that smarty-pants head of yours. Once I get us down, I'll radio for help and see what I can do on the engine. Nothing some elbow grease can't fix. Worst case, we'll be stranded for an hour or two, day tops."

"A day?"

Anxiety clawed at Amelia. She wished he would stop spitting his seeds so nonchalantly. The ocean swelled beneath them while the plane's altitude dropped. Even as Hank held it steady, they could only glide for so long before the ocean kissed their floats.

"Whhoooaaa there, girl!"

Water splashed around the plane in thick curtains like unfurling swan wings. The wet blanket coupled with the setting sun threw the cabin into darkness until the water drained away. Moments later, they came to sway and bob with whatever momentum they had left.

"Well, here we are!" Hank announced with a phlegmy chuckle. "Exits can be found to your left and right. Please watch your step as you exit the craft, as it may be slippery."

Amelia was not amused. Outside her window, the ocean was far darker up close. Even in the orange glow of twilight, its surface looked black. Thinking about the miles of open unknown, swirling beneath them, made her nauseous.

"Er… Here." Turning around, Hank found a lifejacket behind his seat. "You're free to wear this if you want."

She couldn't accept it soon enough. Snapping the ratty preserver around her torso brought a strange sense of security, that if she were to somehow perish, it wouldn't be by drowning.

Hank's door opened as he hefted a small toolbox from under his seat. His stepping outside caused the plane to rock.

"Where are you going?" Amelia cried out, grabbing a handle as she felt ready to tumble through the door and into the ocean.

"To try and fix my engine! You hang tight. I don't wanna be searchin' for ya if you fall out. Gonna be darker than pitch soon enough."

The door was left open, leaving Amelia alone in the cabin. Hank's shifting weight caused the world to lurch as he made his way to a small step welded to a strut. Opening a hinged door over the engine released a plume of smoke. A flurry of clanking metal and curse words followed as Hank checked various parts while trying to hold a flashlight. However, it was all drowned out by the ocean.

Amelia could only hear the water lapping against the floaters, like a dozen hands trying to pull their plane into the depths. Shadows shifted beneath the surface with malicious intent. She knew it was only her imagination, but this didn't stop images of unknown creatures from flooding her mind.

"Wait, did you call anyone on the radio? Shouldn't we tell someone what happened before it gets any darker?"

A collision sent a solid strike through the plane's frame and brought Amelia's neck hair to stand on end. In the middle of the Indian Ocean, she was at a loss for what could have struck them like a boulder.

"What was that?"

"*Dammit...*" Hank grumbled outside, taking little notice.

"Hank..." Amelia called, tightening her lifejacket.

He couldn't hear through the window.

Something struck the plane's passenger right floater

with enough force to tilt the craft several feet. Amelia's eyes widened at what looked like a monstrous body moving through the inky waters.

"Hank!" she called out. *"Can you call for help on the radio first? There's something out there!"*

His hand waved in the glass. "I don't think we need to! Looks like a hose just blew off. Can you grab the jug of coolant under my seat? If we're lucky, the engine didn't seize up!"

It was difficult to hear Hank's words over the water. In the back of her mind, Amelia trembled as she thought she heard a guttural rumble from the ocean.

"Got my coolant?" Hank called, looking through the windshield.

Amelia found her voice. "S-Sure!"

Unbuckling her seatbelt felt like a death wish. Twisting around, she searched the back of the small cabin for the jug.

"Got it!" she yelled out. Like a cat on an unsteady platform, she moved slowly to his open door. Hank's arm extended toward her in anticipation. "Here you–"

The world tilted violently. Metal creaked where joint welds strained as the plane heaved.

"AHH!"

Amelia's heart stopped as the plane was lifted onto its left side, turning the inside of the cabin into a slide leading directly into the ocean. She didn't try to keep a hold of the jug, instead allowing it to tumble through the open door as she scrambled to clutch at the seat and fight against gravity.

"Whatcha go and do that for?" Hank yelled, gripping the side of the plane. *"We don't want to be out here if the waves are picking up enough to–"*

A wind-splitting shriek cut him off. Staring into the

black abyss, Amelia caught sight of a large serpent-like face gliding beneath the water. It resembled a massive great white's head before leading into a thick, elongated mass, slithering back into the depths. The pale lifeless eyes and overgrown teeth would haunt her forever.

"There's no need to yell! I–"

"THERE'S *SOMETHING* OUT THERE!" Amelia screamed. As the plane settled, she hurried back into her seat and the safety of her belt.

"What on earth are you–"

"*I saw it! THERE'S SOMETHING IN THE WATER! It's trying to tip the plane!*"

Hank looked around before staring at the hysterical woman. "What in God's name are you talking about? There's no fish out here bigger than a–"

The plane heaved into the air like a toy. Enduring the sensations of a rollercoaster, Amelia felt sick as they free-fell back to Earth amid a plume of water.

Sea sprayed from their reentry. The plane's frame creaked at the forces. Trash littered the area after tumbling from Hank's open door. Drenched head to toe, Amelia shivered in her seat in shock.

"*Help! HELP!*"

Panic danced over the waves. Amelia looked up to find the seaplane's engine unattended. Hank's dim outline thrashed in the open ocean a dozen yards away.

"*Help me!*"

Against her better judgment, she left the safety of her seat. Darkness descended as she stepped from the cabin and placed a foot on the passenger-side floater. Amelia refused to release her iron grip on Hank's dangling seatbelt as she leaned over the water and extended an arm. The water churned beneath the plane, as if boiling with activity. Even out of the corner of her eyes, Amelia could see monstrous shadows in the blackness.

"Come on! *COME ON!*" she yelled.

"Throw me the lifejacket!"

Sacrificing the preserver was not something she was willing to do. "YOU CAN MAKE IT! JUST SWIM AND–"

A burst of water flung into the twilight sky. For a brief moment, Amelia and Hank saw a scaly tail lash from the depths. It whipped a dozen meters through the air before coming down on top of the pilot. The spray nearly threw Amelia from her slippery perch.

"Hank?" There was no sign of him as the water calmed. Amelia stared out, not daring to move.

"Gwaahhh!"

An arm burst forth, followed by a gasping man. Blood poured down his face from a head wound, though there was no pain in his eyes… only terror. He was treading water in a fight for his life. Amelia's mind was flooded with images of Hank's feet beating relentlessly as miles upon miles of black unknown stretched beneath him.

The horror on his face couldn't have been more vivid. "Oh God! *Oh God!* It's *everywhere!* IT'S GODDAMN *EVERYWHERE! I SAW IT!"*

He neared the plane. Ten yards away, his rescue was plausible. Hank's efforts seemed likely to cause a heart attack, a death more acceptable than whatever awaited him below.

Amelia reached out. "You're almost there! Keep going!"

The world was dead to Hank. He couldn't hear, nor taste, nor smell. He had only one sense: survival. An arm reached out to Amelia as he thrashed in desperation.

"Don't let it get me! DON'T LET IT–"

He slipped under the water in an instant. The motion was so fluid and gentle that Amelia was left wondering if Hank had ever been there at all. Sudden cessation of his horrified cries left a dull ringing in Amelia's ears. Her mind couldn't process his vanishment.

"H… Hank…?" she squeaked, as if hoping he could hear her with several hundred meters of water between them.

He would not resurface a second time.

The sun set, leaving only a dull purple glow to illuminate the western sky as a sheet of stars encroached from the east. Even up close, it was too dark to see what shadows lurked in the waters.

Amelia swallowed. Her heart felt ready to jump from her chest. "H-Hank…?" she called again, hopelessly. Never had the world felt so still.

The plane jolted at an underwater collision. It was Amelia's turn to fight for her life. Scrambling into the cabin to lay across the floor, she grabbed at the radio. Squeezing the microphone illuminated the radio to paint the cabin a sick green.

"Hello? *Hello! Is anyone there?*"

Static came in response amid roiling waters outside. Amelia pulled her feet into the cabin as an extra precaution.

"We crashed! I'm in a seaplane about a hundred miles east of Madagascar! We were heading to Merime! Something ate the pilot! Please send help! *There's something in the water! THERE'S SOMETHING IN THE WATER!*"

The creature rammed the plane's underbelly, throwing Amelia around the cabin like a ragdoll. Her ears rang when she came to rest on the floor.

Frigid water lapped at her feet. Recoiling, she found the

plane's left side sinking into the surf. Bubbles streamed from a ruptured floater. Amelia grabbed for support as water swallowed the plane. Hank's door opened to the vast ocean below. Waiting as a void of darkness beneath Amelia's dangling feet, she knew falling now meant death.

Her eyes scanned the sinking cabin while her ears threatened to pop at the pressure. Jostled open from the last collision, a panel on the underside of the dashboard had fallen to reveal an emergency flare gun. Being her only choice of weapon, Amelia greedily took the tool before straddling the steering wheel and pilot seat.

Opening her door above her head would release the cabin's pressure. She knew she would have only seconds before the plane sank. Flare gun in her mouth, she turned the handle and pushed upward.

Air rushed around her from the approaching floor of water below. It grabbed at Amelia's feet as she climbed onto the side of the overturned seaplane. Its remaining wing protruded into the air like a monument as she stood on the cabin. Water lapped at her shoes with sunflower seeds dotting the surface. In the distance were the remains of the other wing, snapped off after the last attack. She prayed the remaining floater would stay intact.

All was still. Slowly her eyes grew accustomed to the waning light. Water sloshed from drifting sources like whispering specters.

Amelia spun around. Long, smooth bulges deformed the ocean's surface around the sinking plane. The creature was circling her. A black void swirled at her feet.

"Stay the *fuck* away from me!" she screamed, raising the flare gun to point at the water. It wouldn't do much, but it was better than nothing.

A rolling mound of water approached around her right. The flash of a pale-gray pupilless eye as large as her torso stared from below several inches of water. A piece of tattered fabric matching Hank's shirt waved from between two razor teeth. The daggers stuck from its eel-like jaw in an abomination of nature.

Amelia pulled the trigger. Bright red light bathed the area in a bloody sheet. Her aim proved true as the flare struck the beast in the face, though there was little reaction other than its head dipping away.

The flare hissed when it sank. Heart pounding, Amelia looked over the floater's edge into the glowing water below. Hank's terror suddenly made sense.

The monster coiled deep into the abyss. For miles, its body seemed to wind and stretch downward in a tangle of deep-sea death. Even as the flare sank lower, its dimming red sphere never ceased to illuminate the writhing monstrosity plunging into the darkness like a whirlpool.

Amelia fell into a trance at the sight. Watching it circle in a swirling vortex pulled her consciousness from her body. She thought it had to have been a swarm of many smaller creatures, but she could never spy a break in its body. The sheer scale made her tremble with utter despair and she let the gun fall from her grasp.

To enter the water was to invite death.

The flare flickered far below as the ocean grew still. Not even its lively existence could survive the crushing depths.

Something moved from the deepest reaches. In the last moments of the flare's life, Amelia was certain she saw a toothy grimace hurling upward like a rising mountain.

It wasn't the monster that had eaten Hank. This was much larger. It was gray, ancient, and hulking. The maw more closely resembled the gaping mouth of a cave lined with teeth. Scars carved deep gashes into its skin from battles with beasts Amelia didn't want to imagine.

For a moment, the world didn't draw breath.

Chaos erupted on all sides. Caught in the middle of a flailing beast, Amelia was thrown from the plane as the swirling forces tore it apart. She struggled to stay afloat in the black water. Bubbles churned and tried to pull her under despite the help of a lifejacket.

Amelia gagged on mouthfuls of saltwater. All around her, she witnessed arching segments of a hidden serpent's body rise from the surface in a writhing, thrashing dance. She was but a leaf in the middle of a cataclysmic battle of titans.

Energy left the beast in an instant. Falling like crumbling buildings, the scaly arches crashed into the sea with thunderous splashes before all fell silent.

Amelia gasped for air out of persisting horror. Her legs beat furiously looking for any foothold but found only water. The thought of miles of water separating her soles from the titans island-sized jaws drove Amelia into a panic.

The monster sank from view. Lifeless, its coiling body slipped into the deep. Gouges ripped through its sides. Some pieces had been completely severed from others and floated by in colossal fleshy chunks before sinking. Pale moonlight revealed a thick red substance spreading through the water. Its taste stung Amelia's tongue and burned the back of her throat.

She clutched at her lifejacket. It never felt so imprisoning as she fought to catch her breath. She wanted to scream but couldn't find the sanity to do so.

Junk littered the area from what buoyant objects had escaped Hank's plane. Watching the last of the creature's lifeless body sink out of sight, Amelia prayed someone had heard her hurried plea over the radio. Whatever had attacked them, it was nothing compared to the horrors waiting even deeper in the dark depths below her dangling feet.

About *In the Deep*

I was polling friends about horror story ideas, and one of them, a friend with thalassophobia, suggested I write a story about the open ocean. There's not much more to In the Deep *than that; I just made it a personal goal to scare him as much as possible. At one point or another, we've all wondered what's swimming beneath our feet as we float above the dark nothingness. Hopefully, I made you feel a sliver of that same panic while lying in bed.*

Subterranean

THE old dump was finally mine. Not that I had ever particularly wanted it, but the legal process to gain ownership after my grandfather's death was somewhat grueling. I wasn't certain if I should feel a sense of accomplishment or solemnity.

I stood before the house with an expression of disdain. It was more of a shack than a modern home. In my youth, I remember it looking far more majestic and full of adventure. The town itself was brimming with possibilities for an eight-year-old back then. Now, Boulder City was just an old mining town turned into a tourist trap. Updates had been made to bring it into the twenty-first century, like adding an ice cream parlor or renovating the old brothel into a semi-decent hotel. But when all was said and done, it remained just a dusty old town a few miles into the Rockies.

My grandfather had actually inherited this house from his father. It wouldn't have been much in the town's heyday. But over the years, my grandfather saw fit to turn it into a proper abode, with a second floor and some form of plumbing.

Woof! Woof!

I pulled at the leash in my hand. My old lab was making eyes at a terrier across the street. Its owners had tied it to a pole while they went into a small museum to enjoy some AC.

"June, quiet," I hushed, tugging firmly. It was usually enough to bring her back in line. Turning back to the old house, I asked, "So, what do you think? Caught a lot of snakes around here when I was little..."

She didn't respond other than to shake her head. Not sure what I expected. She had no way of knowing how much time I spent running around the property as a kid with my cousins. It may not have been pretty, but it did offer my family a nice getaway in the summer. My grandfather was more than happy to have the extra company for a weekend or two.

I squinted at the siding. Some parts were rotted with visible termite damage. The porch sagged from years of neglect. Likely, it hadn't been built properly in the first place. Old Grandpa just needed somewhere to drink his beers in the shade.

I sighed and approached my new property. "Gonna take a lot more than a coat of paint to get this place ready to sell."

Pushing open the front door made me nervous about the structure's integrity. Groans came from hinges long neglected. The interior was dark and musty. Curtains were drawn across the windows, denying access to the mountain sun. The place was lived in and not well cleaned. Couldn't have been from abandonment; my grandfather had only died three weeks ago. Saddened me to think, I only remember it being so clean because my grandma was alive back then.

You couldn't pay me to sleep on the recliner or sofa in the front room. I could only imagine what the bedroom upstairs was like. Likely, no one had been in there since they found his body. I had every intention of staying at the hotel every night I was here.

His love of fishing covered the walls. Prize-winning taxidermied trout and salmon stared with lifeless eyes between the faded pieces of art. Every creaking floorboard made you think one of the fish might be startled into flopping around on their mounts.

The kitchen was as basic as you could get. A single-burner stove next to a sink was all he needed. Some of the pans looked like they had managed to stick around from when Boulder City was first founded. I prayed the hotel had some form of kitchen or food service.

Woof!

"June! Hush!" I saw her leaning on the window to stare at the terrier. Should have left her at home with the wife.

The hallways seemed so much bigger three decades ago. Now, it felt like my shoulders had only a few inches of clearance on either side. Heading through a back hall toward the bathroom, I paused at a door. It stood out among the rest of the house. Not worn like the others, it sat dark and heavy. I could tell just from a glance that it was made from solid wood.

The basement waited beyond. Even now, it's managed to make my heart flutter. If Grandpa ever caught one of us near it, he quickly shooed us away. No matter how sneaky my cousins and I tried to be, the basement evaded our inspection. We were always told it was because the stairs were old and dangerous.

"Always keep the basement locked," I whispered, standing before the frame. My grandfather had reminded me of this time and time again, to the point where I couldn't walk by the door without hearing his words. Seemed like an odd rule if the stairs were the problem.

This spurred wild theories among my cousins. Ideas and stories about what could possibly be waiting behind the door. I remember us meeting in the trees behind the property to talk in hushed tones about the ghastly noises one of us had apparently heard on the other side. Others shared rumors about Grandpa taking animals into the basement to never be seen again. They always joked he was sacrificing them for some kind of ritual. I was too young to partake in these discussions, other than to listen with wide eyes and agree with whatever they said.

These were nothing more than the ramblings of children, of course. Still, as I stood in that dimly lit hallway staring at the heavy wooden door, I was apprehensive even after all these years. Would Grandpa roll in his grave if I tried to open it?

It was my house now, after all. I had a right to every inch of the place. I reached out to grab the knob with more anxiety than I cared to admit. It rattled in my grasp.

My grandfather's voice didn't yell from over my shoulder. True to his words though, the door had indeed remained locked, right up until he kicked the bucket. As my first order of business, I decided it was high time I found out what was so important.

The attorney had given me a rusty keyring with only three keys. One fit the front door, another I knew fit the propane shed out back, and the last was for a mailbox. None came close to fitting the bill of that gaping metal hole. Grandpa could have been buried with the key for all I knew. I grumbled with a frown.

June was staring at me from the end of the hall. The heat was making her pant. I couldn't deny it was getting to me too. Hopefully, Grandpa had installed an AC.

"This is why I packed power tools and a crowbar. Don't you worry; I'm getting in there one way or another," I promised.

I returned with enough leverage to open a bank vault. I

didn't care if that door was two inches thick; I was getting in. Whatever remained of my childhood whimsey demanded answers.

The crowbar was the first method I tried. It wedged firmly between the door and the frame. I had hoped the frame was rotted enough that it would give way and I could save the door, but even with my full weight the door wouldn't budge. Apparently, keeping this door locked had been important enough for Grandpa to reinforce the frame as well.

After that, I decided it wasn't worth trying to be delicate. I grabbed a hatchet from my toolbox.

Splinters flew with every strike. June scrambled out of the hall after the first whack. Desire fueled my quest for this life-long secret as I swung until sweat covered my brow. Carving deep gashes around the handle, I worked to simply remove the lock from the door altogether.

Darkness started showing through the other side. It looked like a rabid beaver had gnawed a crescent moon around the handle. Grinning like a child on Christmas, I plunged my crowbar into the splinters and pushed.

Sounds of splitting wood filled the hall. It bowed and bucked in a losing battle. Listening to it pop, I gave a final push through the security. The door splintered open and swung to dent the wall. I huffed in triumph and pulled the handle from the door frame before tossing it down the hall as a piece of junk.

Darkness waited in front of me. The stairs indeed looked old, but not enough to warrant concern. They descended into the inky blackness, as if there were an ocean in the basement. Years of must and moisture reached my nostrils. I recoiled at the scent of rancid death. A light switch from the last century waited along the inner wall. Pressing the button brought two lights to life: one above the stairs and one in the middle of the basement below.

Subconsciously taking extra care down the stairs, I entered the lower level. June's curious feet tapped on the stairs behind me to see what all the excitement was about. Her wagging tail brought an odd sense of comfort to the dreary room.

I couldn't believe how ordinary it all looked. A workbench sat along the back wall under the center of the house. Shelves of motor oils, paints, and various rusted tools lined most of the walls. Two barrels of, what I assumed to be, homemade wine sat in a corner. One wall however, was particularly interesting and it lent some truth to my cousins' claims.

Situated against the wall on the back of the house was a door. I had never seen a door so well reinforced. Lined with metal bracers, it made the basement door look like it was made of cardboard. There was no getting through this door with a hatchet.

To the right was a long wooden table. A butcher block sat on one end, carved deep with the gouges of a missing blade. Dark brown stains of animal blood had permeated the grain. Some of it looked as recent as my grandfather's death. A few straggling chicken feathers peppered the floor.

He was down here before he died, possibly within a few days.

I snapped my fingers at June as she jumped up to sniff the block. *"Hey!* Get away from there." She obeyed but licked her chops all the same at the intriguing scents.

A bloody butcher block wasn't enough to keep my attention. Boulder City was an old mining town and not exactly near a supermarket. Was Grandpa killing animals for ritualistic sacrifice like my cousins thought? Probably not. Killing them for food? Most likely.

The door, however, pulled me in like a magnet. Maybe the reason for the secrecy wasn't the basement, but whatever was behind this daunting door anchored into the stone of the mountain.

A padlock blocked my advancement. I had only seen locks like this in old Westerns. The thing was bigger than my hand and felt heavier than ten pounds. I would need an hour with a hacksaw to cut through its shackle. Or… one well-placed hit with the sledgehammer sitting in the corner. The sound made the basement ring like a bell when I brought the hammer down.

Apparently, age had gotten the better of the lock. Though the shackle remained whole, the internal mechanisms broke apart at my strike. I smiled while removing the broken lock from the door and tossing it across the room. Perhaps a hundred years ago, it was better at keeping people out.

The sound the door made when I swung it open on its rock-mounted hinges made my bones rattle. I felt the temperature drop immediately. The basement was a sauna compared to the gaping darkness within this tunnel. It reminded me of looking into the basement for the first time, only now, there was no light switch along the wall.

June whined from the base of the stairs. I guess it was

unsettling for her as well.

A sudden bark in warning made me jump. Her soundwaves dove into the tunnel and bounced off the walls like a bullet before fading off into the depths of the mountain. It was like dropping a stone down a well and waiting for it to hit the water. The longer I listened, the more apprehensive I became standing at the entrance.

There were abandoned mineshafts all across these mountains. I could hardly drive anywhere without seeing them along the road. In old mining towns like Boulder City, it wasn't uncommon for some shacks or houses to be built over the existing mining structures. I pondered the possibility for a moment. It made sense why children wouldn't be allowed in a basement with a mineshaft. It made more sense than dangerous stairs at least.

I stepped into the tunnel. A flight of steps was hewn into the rock before fading out of the basement's light. The tunnel walls struck me as odd. They didn't look like they had been carved by pickaxes. There were some deep gouges in groups of three or four, though they were too elongated for me to attribute to any specific tool.

Armed with a flashlight, I stepped into the tunnel and bid June wait for my return. I counted fifteen stairs before the tunnel leveled out. It was wide enough for someone to walk comfortably, though the headroom left something to be desired. The tunnel continued only for a time before branching into three new paths. I took the right-most for the sake of simplicity. This is where I began to comprehend the scale of what lay before me.

There was no end to the tunnels. My flashlight shined as best it could, but the darkness was thick. There were always more corridors. More opportunities to lose my way. I had kept to the right so far, but it was easy to imagine myself becoming hopelessly lost in the chilly subterranean world.

I turned around. It was uncomfortable walking with the vast expanse of unknown at my back. Given how far these tunnels could go, I didn't like thinking about what I could have turned my back on.

Returning to my grandfather's basement felt like returning to my own world. June was still waiting for me and more than excited to see my return. I responded with gentle ear scratches while pondering what I'd stumbled across. It certainly wasn't a mineshaft. It was something else entirely. I had always heard legends of lost Native American civilizations sprawled beneath our feet. Until now, I never gave them much credit. But why was it in my grandfather's basement?

I had to know more. Searching the piles of tools, I found a large coil of paracord, easily several thousand feet in length. It wouldn't let me explore everything, but it would keep me from getting lost. I clamped a large screwdriver into my grandfather's vice and set the spool on top before tying the end to my belt loop.

"June! Come here!" I whistled.

She stared at me from under the butcher's table. There was fear in her eyes, and I could hear her whimpering. The open door to the tunnel wasn't sitting well with her, but I wasn't about to leave her unattended in the old house.

"June, *come*," I said more sternly.

Head down, she approached. With the leash clicked to her collar, we stood in front of the labyrinth together. For the first time in thirty years, I felt the same excitement as when I was a child.

I tucked a revolver in the back of my jeans as an extra precaution. I was adventurous, but not a fool. Who knew what kind of snakes or badgers might be living there.

"Let's see what the rest of our basement looks like," I urged June. She wasn't as excited as me but followed closely abreast. It was rare not to see her leading.

The paracord tugged at my jeans with every step. It became harder to move when I rounded corners, but my curiosity wouldn't let the friction get the better of me.

The underground was far more complex than I anticipated. As I delved deeper, found more flights of stairs and branching tunnels, I became more and more certain that some form of intelligent beings had indeed created these walls. It couldn't have been miners in search of gold.

There was a reasoning to this dark work. I was surrounded by remnants of a civilization long since extinct. I walked among its ruins with only my flashlight as a guide, revealing illuminated conical sections of the, otherwise, pitch-black void. Without it, I might as well have been blind. The rope at my back was my greatest source of comfort. Its tugging was a constant consolation that I could find my way back to the surface. Echoes of my own footsteps left me wallowing in the sensation of being followed. I'm not ashamed to admit to looking over my shoulder several times.

There were countless small alcoves and rooms. I was frightened when I saw the first, indicated only by a small doorway carved into the stone. My mind tricked me into thinking I saw a face through the opening, but I knew better. A glimpse inside revealed what I believed to be some kind of storage space. There was some debris on the floor, what looked to be pieces of broken pottery and wood.

Other nooks followed this same pattern. Sometimes they would have large open windows looking into the tunnel, or smoothed boulders arranged in a circle or lining the walls. Chairs perhaps?

The deeper I dared to go, the faster my heart raced. Every flight of stairs taunted me to go just a little further. There was some art on the walls, but my flashlight wasn't bright enough to let me see it clearly. The markings reminded me of petroglyphs, though these were unlike any I had seen above ground.

June stopped suddenly to sniff the air. I felt my blood freeze in my veins when I feared we had stumbled across a bear, but then I felt a gentle breeze. The smell of charred meat found my nostrils. My flashlight swung toward the ceiling. There I spied a small chute heading far into the rock above. Was I somewhere near the burger restaurant in Boulder City? Whoever had built this maze had been smart enough to build air ducts. My best guess was this one let out along the side of the mountain near the restaurant, likely hidden beneath the brush. How someone could accomplish such a feat without modern tools left me baffled.

"I think we should get a burger after this, eh, June?" I chuckled. "That smell is making my mouth water even under a mountain."

Sometimes the tunnels met with gaping crevices, cutting through the inside of the mountain. My meager flashlight had no hope of penetrating that darkness. Some of them spanned before me like a tear through the world itself. Thinking about slipping into those chasms made me uncomfortably dizzy at their edges, and I would have to back away with both feet firmly on the ground.

I never would have had the courage to explore to such an extent without the rope at my back. Thinking about the amount of rock hanging above my head was nerve-wracking. That, plus the ever-groping darkness at my back and shoulders, was enough for my heart. The possibility of getting lost didn't need to be tossed into the mix.

The reality of my exploration hit when the tether pulled taut at my jeans. A gentle yank hoped to dislodge it from a particularly rough wall. I couldn't have gone the full length already. There was still so much to explore! My hand tugged again as June started to whine at my side.

"It's alright, girl," I grunted, pulling again.

June's whines echoed down the tunnels. Her head spun between two branching paths ahead. I could hear some shifting rocks but was too busy adjusting my tether to think much of it. Maybe if I had paid more attention to June's anxiety and the tail between her legs, things would have gone differently.

She growled. This caught my interest. More rocks clattered further down the tunnel, too far for my flashlight to reveal.

Woof… woof woof!

June lashed out, almost pulling the leash from my hands. Her teeth bared themselves to the chilly air. Her hackles stood on end. I had never seen her so riled up.

"J-June! June, calm down, *dammit!*"

My hands burned between holding onto her leash and the rope at my back.

WOOF!

She was in a frenzy. This was a dog in full attack mode. My hand started to slip.

"JUNE! HEEL! HEEL!"

A sound made the blood curdle in my veins. It split the air like the cry of a distressed rabbit followed by strong fading clicks. The tunnel reverberated with its screech. Perhaps it was just a small animal meeting its end. Perhaps it was a warning.

I wasn't about to stick around to find out.

Woof WOOF!

"June!" I hissed. *"Come on! We're–"*

Another screech sounded off to drive her mad. I couldn't stop her. My grip wasn't prepared. I knew she was gone the moment her leash slipped from my sweating palms.

"JUNE!"

She ran beyond the range of my flashlight and down a tunnel, barking madly at whatever was with us. I could hear her nails scraping against the stone in the darkness.

I couldn't leave her. Maybe it really was just a rabbit that had wandered in from a burrow. Against every fiber of common sense screaming in my body, I cut the rope from my jeans and gave chase.

"June! June, get back here, *dammit!"*

Her barking echoed from all directions in a twisted dance with those shrill screeches. I didn't know which path to take. How far had she gone? My brain ached from the auditory strobe of her howling.

WOOF!

"June! COME HERE!"

A series of clicks, followed by the yelping of a pained

dog shot through the labyrinth. She'd caught whatever she was chasing. Or worse… it had caught her.

Silence fell within the mountain. I regretted ever entering these tunnels. I'd lost so much in an instant, for the sake of curiosity. Grandpa spoke to me from his grave.

Should have listened to me, boy.

"J… June…?"

I waited, hearing nothing. Anxiety choked the air from my throat like a merciless hand.

"June…!" I called again, noticing my voice becoming shaky.

Woof!

Relief came over me in a cool wave. She wasn't dead. Lost, but not dead. Maybe we could still make it out of this place in one piece.

"June! *Come here, girl!*"

Woof!

Woof!

It wasn't easy finding her in the maze of tunnels. With her voice bouncing off the walls in every direction, I had to focus myself to find the most probable source all while listening for whatever else could be lurking underground. That awful screeching hadn't sounded since she ran off. I prayed she'd managed to chase it away.

I called out again, hoping for another clue. "June…!"

Woof!

Woof! Woof!

She was very close. Any of the nearby corridors or alcoves could be hiding her now.

"*Shhh, girl,*" I hushed. Being this close, I didn't want to risk something else finding us before I could get to her. It would be difficult enough to remember my way back to the end of the rope.

Woof! Woof!

I was right on top of her. Couldn't have been more than a corner or two away. All I had to do was grab her leash and turn back. I was ready to be done with this place. Hearing her barking around a bend, I turned into a small hallway and cast my flashlight across the floor.

"Ju–"

Her body lay lifeless on the stone. It wasn't difficult to see she'd been dead for a while. My mind reeled, grappling with the seemingly impossible reality. I know I had heard her bark only moments ago, but given the pool of blood, I knew that was impossible.

"J... June?"

Woof!

It came from overhead. Swinging my light upward, I discovered the lurking horror.

A ghoul born of darkness clung to the ceiling. Gray skin covered its lanky figure to make it blend, frighteningly well, into the stone walls. Purple veins ran over its body, some as thick as a pencil. Not a strand of hair grew from the monster. I felt small under its mass. At full height it must have easily exceeded eight feet tall. Those slender white fingers could have wrapped around my head like a spiderweb.

The head was the worst. It overwhelmed my visual senses as my brain tried to reconcile the nightmarish sight with reality. I couldn't tell whether or not it had skin. It looked like the head of a jackal, peeled free of any flesh. There were no lips to hide its gums or teeth. Empty eye sockets stared ahead without life. Globs of saliva fell to June's fur.

Woof! Woof!

Its imitation of June made my spine tremble. It was so perfect, and I had fallen for it without a second thought. Seeing the familiar happy labrador sounds coming from such a fiendish head was enough to make me sick to my stomach.

The beast jumped at me. There was only time to raise my arm in defense before I was on my back. It stood over me on all fours, gnashing for my face. Our limbs tangled together in a desperate dance of predator and prey.

My ears bled from its cry emanating so close. Rapidly clamping jaws chomped at the air in front of my eyes. Spittle coated my face. I tried to push its body away, but my hands just slid against the slippery gray hide. It was strong. Fighting it was a death wish. Knowing my end would come soon, I raised my forearm in front of my face and allowed the creature to bite down.

"NNGH!"

Bones snapped between its jaws. It seared like acid but I couldn't pull away. Sacrificing my arm, I sought the revolver in my pocket. Blood stung my eyes when I pressed the barrel into the monster's torso.

I emptied five rounds into that cursed beast's body, each one muffled by its flesh at point-blank range. I couldn't use my last shot; if I was caught, I didn't want my death to be by those nightmarish vice grips. The resulting shriek made the pain in my arm worth the torture. It brought a strange sense of consolation to see it was capable of feeling pain. With such a demonic figure, part of me was scared it could be impervious to such earthly sensations.

It scrambled away with blood draining profusely from a

gaping tear on its side. The blood didn't smell like any I had ever encountered from hunting. This thing was barely an animal. Even more troubling was the amount of life left within its form. I only watched it screech and writhe for a second before I knew my revolver had failed to do a lethal amount of damage.

I ran with my arm clutched to my chest. Blood soaked through my shirt and I could feel deep puncture wounds big enough for my index finger to enter. I would be lucky to keep the limb after this excursion. There wasn't time to think about that right now; worrying about keeping a limb was a luxury for the living.

I could already hear more coming.

An ear-piercing howl vibrated through my chest, as if searching for my heart. I nearly slipped when I turned on my heel and sprinted down the tunnel.

Why did I remove my rope? I was safe with it at my back! It could have gotten me out of this subterranean hell! Everything looks the same! I can't navigate without it!

The thing was scrambling after me in the darkness behind my back. Dastardly feet and hands scraped against the floor and walls. I don't think I could outrun it, even on flat ground in daylight. But trapped under a mountain in cramped tunnels? I didn't stand a chance.

Their clicking was closer than ever. Watching me scramble away... The clattering jaws of that naked skull sounded like it was right at the nape of my neck. I didn't have the courage to shine the light behind me. Every step forward was a step closer to the exit.

Woof!

Woof woof!

It was trying to trick me. Lure me back in. I couldn't fall

for it. I couldn't let myself think it was possible even for a second. I'm sorry, June; I never meant for this to be where you spent your last moments. You deserved better than to die alone, terrified, and lost in the darkness.

My flashlight strobed around the tunnel with my pumping hands. I was disoriented. I was lost. I had no way of knowing if I was even headed in the right direction or going deeper into this underground prison.

A hallway approached on my left. Feet sliding across the floor, I dove into the passage. The beast screamed at the unexpected change in my path and skidded past the entrance. I had a chance, but only a few seconds before it was over. Spying an empty room, I jumped through a window and huddled myself against the wall by the door.

My flashlight shut off. I don't know how it sensed its prey, but I wasn't taking any chances. Pure darkness washed over me. I never knew it could be so utterly, completely black. It hurt my eyes to stare into that void beneath a mountain. Somehow the back of my eyelids seemed brighter compared to my surroundings.

The silence was deafening. It didn't last long before I heard my pursuer clicking nearby.

Echolocation. It knew I was hiding. The pale form crept through the tunnel with slow, investigative movements. It was searching for me just outside the room.

Its jaws clacked and echoed down the tunnels. I was being hunted by a demonic cave skeleton that could see in the dark. Feeling its vibrations run over my body made me bristle. Every solid jolt of air rattled my skull.

It loosed a low, guttural scream. My heart lurched into my throat. It was at the doorway. Its searching noises bounced around the room. I couldn't see it, but I could hear its raspy breath only a foot away.

The air was colder around its body. Frost might have formed on the wall behind me. It walked on all fours like a coyote with legs too long for its body. My heart had never been so loud as when I felt its face come within inches of mine. The breath from its mouth reeked of rotten earth and blood.

BEEP BEEP!

I was going to die. My watch sounded, alerting me that it was the turn of the hour. Doing so made the face illuminate with a dull green glow. It cast itself upon the beast's face, showing the bony visage like a ghost floating in the darkness.

The jaws angled toward me. Shadows cast into its empty eye sockets. Strands of drool stretched several inches before landing on the ground and my hand. I spied bloody clumps of dog hair stuck between its teeth, and I wanted to scream. I prayed my watch would turn off. I couldn't stand to stare at this monstrosity for another second, but I didn't know if it would be able to sense my eyes closing.

Fully entering the room, its jaw hovered within inches of my face. I could have kissed it if I was mad enough. Staring it down, eye to eye, I was certain it had found me. As my watch light faded and left me in the all-consuming darkness, I waited for those hidden jaws to grab my neck.

A screech reverberated from the maze's depths. Rearing up, my pursuer stared out the window above me. Someone else had found its half-eaten kill. My poor June.

An angry set of clicks and it was gone. Chips of rock pelted me when it lunged at the wall and crawled out the window to the top of the tunnel outside. I listened for a minute, those claws scraping the ceiling before it finally faded away.

Silence enveloped me once more. This was my chance. Covering the end of my flashlight with my hand, I clicked it on and made sure there wasn't still a toothy jackal standing over me.

I was alone for the time being. My flashlight illuminated the room. It was empty save for some chicken bones. I was just glad I hadn't turned on the light to find a pile of human skulls at this point. Aiming the beam toward the doorway brought the real surprise.

My rope! It was there, lying limp in the tunnel. By pure fortune, I had managed to circle back around! I had a chance. My revolver was cold in my hand when I removed it from my waistband. I didn't intend on being killed with bullets in the chamber. Listening for any final sign of the beasts, I grabbed the paracord and began sprinting in the direction of resistance.

The tunnels moved in amorphous blurs of light and dark while I ran. Unable to keep my light still while running, the illumination bounced in a rapid pattern fast enough to make me nauseous. If I died here, my body would not be found. My screams would not be heard. I would simply vanish from the world, like whatever ancient civilization built this network of tunnels in the first place.

A pale limb flashed in the corner of my eye. They were closing in. Instinctively, I took a madman's aim with the revolver and pulled the trigger while running.

I cursed my decision a second later. Though the thing fell back, the gunshot roared through the tunnel like a clap of thunder inside my head. I instantly went deaf. My ears rang in anger. Were they all calling out to each other now? Was I being chased? I couldn't hear my own footsteps, let alone their ghostly wails, but I could smell clean air and the scent of freshly grilled burgers. I was near the exit.

I scrambled, rope in hand. It felt like there were claws reaching at my shirt. There wasn't time to figure out if they were real. I would know later if I took it off and found it in tatters.

There was dim light ahead. It burned my eyes after so long in the tunnels, but I wanted to cry tears of joy. It washed over the initial flight of stairs like a golden glow of salvation leading out of this hellscape.

I couldn't hear myself gasping for air as I scrambled up the stone steps. I fell twice, each time fearing something would grab my ankle and pull me back down. Running through the reinforced door must have looked like I was finishing a race. Only now, did I notice the web of gouges on the back of the door.

It shook against my hands when I threw it shut. There was nothing to hold it closed. No handle, no lock after I had broken it. Desperate, I stuck a screwdriver into the latch.

The basement jolted at my feet. Something had rammed the other side with enough force to bend the screwdriver. It was never going to hold. Backing away, I found the stairs leading into the house.

I knew they must have been screaming. I was glad I couldn't hear them over the ringing in my ears. Scrambling up the stairs on all fours, I reached the hallway.

The basement door slammed shut only to bounce off the frame and creak open. The handle was gone, as was the lock. The jagged hole made by the hatchet mocked me.

The screwdriver snapped and clattered to the basement floor in fragments. The door flung open to the tunnels below. It stood motionless before pale ghoulish figures emerged from the darkness. Maybe if I had paid attention to the claw marks on the back of the door, I would have thought twice about venturing into the abyss. Their approaching screams came muffled through my ringing ears, rising from a horde of ghouls emerging from the earth.

I should have kept the basement locked.

About *Subterranean*

Have you heard of Derinkuyu? It's a vast, 1000-year-old, underground city that was discovered in 1963 beneath Turkey. The tunnels extend almost 100 meters down for a total of eighteen different levels. There are houses, wells, a ventilation system, and even stables! They estimate it housed around 20,000 people.

Derinkuyu provided a lot of inspiration for this story, both in design and mystique. The sheer scale of the city blows my mind. Like the tunnels in Subterranean, Derinkuyu was even discovered in an elderly man's basement while he was doing renovations. It goes to show that while these are fictional tales of horror, they're not completely disconnected from reality. Sprawling networks of tunnels do run beneath our feet, and some of them are still waiting in the dark to be unearthed. Keep that in mind the next time you start digging.

The Gap in the Closet

THE gentle motion was hardly noticeable in the midnight darkness. I didn't think anything of it at first; our house was old and things liked to settle. Maybe our cat, Misty, had been pawing at the door after I'd forgotten to fully close it. Still in a cloud of sleep, I rolled over and pulled the blankets to my chin.

Dreamland might have swallowed my consciousness once more if it hadn't been for a whisper from the darkness.

"Caleb…"

Drowsiness must have shielded my ears from such a soft noise. I shifted under the sheets when my calf prickled against an imaginary bug. The open closet wouldn't leave my mind, but I had to ignore it. Twelve years old was far too mature to be scared of an ajar door.

"Caleb…"

The voice was undeniable this time. I opened my eyes to see my desk. A window sat over it, looking out to the cold night beyond. Why did I have to roll over? Why did I put my back toward my closet? I could potentially see the door in the window's reflection, but I didn't dare let my eyes focus enough to do so.

"Caleb… I have something for you."

It sounded like someone calling to me from underwater.

Fluid filled the spaces between the syllables, as if they were drowning but the words were dry as a desert wind.

Sleep's grasp had left me in favor of a racing pulse. An invisible weight of denial kept me frozen in place. I couldn't bring myself to roll over and face the voice's source.

"Caleb... It's me."

Something like fingernails tapped against the door's inside. Hollow and dry... Why did the voice sound so frighteningly familiar, yet my body was reacting with cold sweats?

"Caleb... Don't you want to kiss your mother goodnight?"

There was movement in the window's reflection. I only saw it for a second: a pale blur moving across the few inches of darkness in my open closet.

Something was in there. It sounded like my mother's voice if she had a mouth full of soggy decaying leaves.

"Caleb... Come here, sweetie."

Sweat covered me like a second sheet. I could feel the bed growing damp under my body. Surely this had to be a dream.

I had to roll over. It went against every instinct screaming in my head. My muscles didn't want to follow my will. I thought I might faint as I forced myself onto my back. Time slowed while the room rotated. Watching the other side of the bed rise into view, left me silently praying.

There was nothing there. No claw nor gruesome face waiting at the edge of my mattress. The relief was almost as great as my fear itself.

There was still the matter of my closet, however. I turned my head to look, finding an empty column of darkness between the door and the frame. There should have been only clothes inside.

Minutes passed without the voice. I began thinking I had awoken from a nightmare without noticing. Only the sounds of an old house were present to keep me company. A distant rumbling came from my parents' room downstairs, surely my dad's snoring. Listening to the constant droning helped bring peace to my racing heart. Soon, my eyes grew heavy. There were no monsters here, only the sound of–

"Caleb."

The blood curdled in my veins. I couldn't look away from the darkness.

Teeth appeared before anything else. More teeth than what felt normal. They spread in a wide, frozen grin refusing to waver. I don't know how her lips could stretch so thin, nor how her grimace could be so visible in my dark closet. There was no light in her eyes. Open wide and refusing to blink, they stared at me from across my room. Her face was pale and shrouded in shadow. Whatever was below her neck vanished into the inky blackness.

It was undoubtedly my mother. Her head was stabilized in my direction with bobbing, cat-like movements.

"Caleb..." she whispered. How she managed to do so with so little lip movement made me shiver. *"You never said goodnight...! Come give me a hug."*

I screamed. Nightmare or not, I wanted this to be over. No twelve-year-old signs up for this.

"MOMMYYYY! MOMMYYYYYYYYY!"

The entire neighborhood was awake when my parents raced to my room. They must have thought I was being murdered. I'd never seen my dad burst through a door so ready for violence.

My light came on and suddenly the terrors of the night were banished. Frantic, my mother rushed to my bedside to coddle her terrified child.

"Sweetie? Sweetie, what is it?" she asked, taking my head in her hands upon finding me so pale.

I stared at the open closet behind her. There was no face in the darkness, but seeing hers so aligned with its last location didn't ease my fright. My imagination ran wild as I expected her lips to stretch and her eyes to stare like a hungry ghoul's.

My dad was less sympathetic upon finding me safe. He sighed and rubbed his tired eyes. "Bad dream, buddy?"

I pointed to the open door. "T-There was a face in the closet!"

Not hesitating, my father opened the door and flicked the switch. Only hanging clothes stared back. No pale face. No frozen grimace. No grating whisper. He closed it in mild annoyance.

Running a hand through my hair, my mom asked, "Did you sneak a snack before bed? You know that gives you nightmares."

"No! I-I–"

"Momma…?"

We turned to find my little sister at my bedroom door. The commotion had dragged her from bed as well, teddy bear and all.

Dad met her head-on. "Go back to bed, cupcake. Caleb just had a bad dream." Picking her up like a doll, he carried her back to her room.

"Everything is alright, sweetie," Mom promised. "Just a nightmare."

Dreams don't open your closet doors. Like any sane child, I always made sure to close mine before turning off the lights. Something else had turned that knob.

A kiss planted itself on my forehead. "Go back to sleep, sweetie. I love you."

"Love you too…" I grumbled.

They were gone as quickly as they arrived. Left to the darkness once more, I closed my eyes and rolled away from the closet. I was far too old to be calling for my mother in the middle of the night. Especially for such a silly dream as–

I heard it open. I didn't need to look; I could feel the empty void. The faint smell of putrid air pricked my nostrils. Unseen, I heard her nails curl around the doorframe.

"Goodnight, sweetie…"

*   *   *

DAYLIGHT has a way of keeping even the night's scariest horrors at bay. I awoke groggier than usual and tumbled out of bed. It was obvious I'd been through a rough night, but I was too tired to remember why. There wasn't time to dwell on dreams when I had to get ready for school.

I approached my closet like a zombie. Only when I extended a hand toward the door did last night come flooding back.

My body recoiled and I stumbled. My chest felt incapable of containing my lungs. The door was still ajar, but there were no whispers, no clacking of nails on wood. I knew it couldn't have been real, but my mind refused to remove that uncanny visage from my memory.

I grabbed a baseball bat and stood away to open the door from a distance. Of course I was scared of what I might find, but I was just as scared of my mother discovering I wasn't dressed for school so late in the morning.

The door opened. Inside were only clothes and some storage bins. There wasn't enough room for an adult to fit inside, much less a monster after my flesh. For good measure I swung the bat into my shirts. There was no monster: only my imagination.

Thanks to my detective work, I was able to completely put the ordeal out of my head. Dreams have a funny way of disappearing if you let something else occupy your mind for more than a few minutes. The face was no different. By the time I was staring into a bowl of sugary cereal, it was less than a forgotten memory.

*　　*　　*

DELIGHTFUL scents of a mother's cooking filled the kitchen when the school bus returned me home. Few memories stay with you like a mother's love filling a pot to the brim.

"Hi, Mom!" I greeted her, abandoning my backpack at the door.

"Welcome home, sweetie! How was school?" She left a bubbling stove unattended to give me a kiss. "Feel like spaghetti and meatballs for dinner?"

Nothing could have been sweeter music to my ears. I quickly nodded and accepted a taste of homemade sauce.

Satisfied with my grin, she ushered me upstairs. "Go get changed and we'll get started on your math homework before your father gets home."

Misty followed me up the stairs, as if I had treats in my socks. Mom hated when I let her get hair all over my school clothes, but I didn't mind. Misty knew how to greet you after being away.

"Caleb?"

I slowed my pace as I entered our upstairs hallway. It sounded like my sister was in my room.

Her voice called again, more annoyed now. "Where'd you go?"

Raising an eyebrow, I entered to find her looking under my bed. "What are you doing in my room?"

Justine popped out in shock. Her brown hair was tangled from rubbing under my bed. *"How did you do that?"*

"Do what?"

"You were calling my name!" Justine came close and narrowed her eyes with all the accusation an eight-year-old could muster. "I *saw* you run in here."

"No, I just got home."

This seemed to stump her. "N… No you didn't. I *SAW* you! You told me to come find you!"

It was too close to dinner time for this. Not wanting to put up with her imagination, I pushed her toward the door. "I think you're seeing things. Now get out; I have to change."

"But–"

I closed my door and sighed. It was getting harder to keep up with her as I got older. Eager to finish my homework before dinner, I started to change but froze halfway across my room.

The closet door was ajar. Had that been one of the places Justine looked? I was certain I had closed it this morning. A sliver of the previous night flashed through my mind. The thought of the event somehow connecting to Justine's experience was far too outlandish to even consider. Still, I was uneasy about approaching the gap.

I felt foolish, but resolved to stay away. A dirty pair of shorts and a t-shirt from the floor wouldn't hurt for one night. I didn't even try to close the door; maybe that's what angered it in the first place.

"Caleb! Don't wait too long to get started on your homework!" Mom's voice came from downstairs.

"Coming…!"

*   *   *

IT was dark by the time I was ready to go to bed. Entering my room was among one of the last things I wanted to do, especially with the sun no longer protecting me from the horrors of the night. If Justine hadn't acted so strangely when I got home from school, maybe the entire ordeal would have remained purged from my mind.

I heard my mom's voice come from the living room. "Go brush your teeth! I'll be up in a few to tuck you in."

Our stairs never seemed so long. I cursed our house for only having one light switch for the upstairs hallway. With Justine gone to bed an hour prior, the second floor was a black abyss where only the unknown awaited me.

My stomach was in knots. I could feel the darkening chill

closing in around me. The hallway ahead stretched into creeping hidden horrors. I didn't dare blink when I reached the landing; the last thing I wanted was to look away from the light switch and find a gruesome face in front of mine.

A click brought the lights on with little fanfare. Of course there was nothing there; this was the real world. I was letting my imagination get the better of me. Feeling my pulse slow, I walked past my room to the bathroom.

It was only a blur, but it was there. Something ran past my door in the darkness. I couldn't be sure what it was; there had only been a brief shadowy outline. It looked humanoid, but its movements were lanky and sloppy as if drunk or hobbled, and it was far too tall and thin to be a person.

I gulped and began to call out, "*J-Justi–*"

A sound like a gunshot rattled my bones. Whatever it was had just sequestered itself back into my closet and slammed the door behind it.

"*Caleb! You're going to wake your sister!*" my mother's voice scolded from downstairs.

I couldn't respond. I had to act now while that thing was in my closet. Slipping my hand around my door frame and into my room, I searched for the light switch.

A golden glow bathed my bed. I kicked my door open to find nothing waiting, though one of my jackets was still swinging from a hook on the outside of my closet door. There was no doubt it had recently moved.

Enough was enough. Whether or not this was only in my head, I wasn't going to put up with it for another night. Taking my desk chair, I wedged it against the floor and my closet handle. Even my dad couldn't have opened that door from the inside now, much less some non-existent specter. Or so I hoped.

Brushing my teeth was more an act of procrastination than hygiene. When every pre-bedtime ritual had been completed, however, there was nothing more I could do to stall.

Mrowl…!

Misty greeted me in the hallway. I think she knew I was struggling with something. Taking the orange furball in my arms brought me comfort as I entered, what should have been, my space.

The chair was still against my closet. The jacket had ceased its movement. Everything looked calm. Making sure to have my bedside lamp on before turning out my light, I flipped the switch and raced to bed.

There was a loud pop with a bright flash. Then darkness lit only by the spots in my vision.

I froze halfway across my room when the lamp bulb burst. Groping darkness smothered me and choked my heart. I don't think my feet touched the ground when I scrambled onto the safety of my mattress. Oblivious to my fears, it didn't take long for Misty to curl up between my legs even as I pulled the covers to my chin.

Darkness huddled around my bed. My room felt like a scene frozen in winter. I didn't want to breathe. Maybe if I held my breath long enough, I would pass out before I had to endure this torment for much longer.

Goosebumps sprang to my skin when the closet door rattled. Misty jolted upright between my legs to stare. Seeing such a reaction wasn't comforting; it meant it wasn't in my head.

The door thunked against the chair. I could see the handle jostling in the darkness and my jacket bouncing up and down. *Something* wanted out.

It tried harder. Efforts doubled. Annoyed desperation shook the door with hurricane force.

I wanted to scream. Misty looked like she was surrounded by exploding firecrackers. Why was this thing tormenting me?

"Caleb…"

"Stop!"

"Open the door, Caleb…"

"GO AWAY!"

"Caleb! What in the world has gotten into you?"

My light came on and stung my eyes. It hadn't been the thing calling my name, but my mother. I was so frightened I hadn't noticed her open my bedroom door. Normally, I should be relieved in her presence, but her face brought fear. I could only see it waiting in the darkness.

"What is going on with you…?" she asked again, worried. A hand placed itself against my forehead. "You're burning up!"

"Mom… Can I sleep downstairs on the couch?"

She stared at me like I'd just asked to spend the night on the roof. "Why would you want to do that?"

My eyes flitted between her and the closet. "I… just can't sleep in here…"

"You just have to turn your mind off. You're thinking so fast that you can't find peace."

"Mom, can I please sleep somewhere else?" I didn't want to let her hear the fear in my voice but I was becoming desperate.

"No, Caleb; you won't sleep well on the couch and then you'll be tired for school. You're sleeping in your room, in your bed." My sentence was sealed with a kiss on my forehead. "Now turn your mind off."

If only it was just my mind. I watched her go to leave before pausing to stare at my closet.

"What in the..." She walked toward my desk chair. "What is this doing here? You're going to hurt yourself if you get up in the middle of the night." My eyes must have looked like moons when she removed the chair from my closet and replaced it under my desk. "Honestly, Caleb, you need to learn to keep your room clean."

My light went off.

"Love you, sweetie. Get some sleep." Looking back a final time, my mom bid me goodnight and closed my door.

Misty settled at my feet before soothing herself with purrs.

Sweat made my pajamas cling to me like a second skin. I stared between my closet and my desk. If I was fast, maybe I could jam the chair again before–

"*Caleb...*"

–it opened. The haunting void stared back, along with a penetrating stench. I knew what was coming, but I couldn't have prepared myself.

"*Caleb... Caleb, sweetie...*"

Her face appeared. The same woman who had just put me to bed was now staring back from my closet. That menacing uncanny grin turned my blood to ice. Why were there so many teeth?

"Caleb… Caleb, come here… I want to kiss you goodnight."

"Go away," I whispered. Was I allowed to confront it? What could happen if I retaliated? If it was able to leave my closet and come for me, wouldn't it have done so already? If it was running around my room earlier, why not now?

"Caleb… Can you help me? I'm stuck."

Misty stared at the closet when I pulled my blanket up to my chin. *"Leave me alone."*

Those tapping, clacking nails were insidious. The rattling against the door turned my blood to ice.

"Caleb," she growled, *"it's rude to speak to your mother that way. Won't you come give your mother a hug?"*

I steeled myself and felt blood rushing through my ears. "You're not my mom."

The face pulled back into the blackness. A dry laugh made me want to vomit.

There was a pause. For a brief, hopeless moment, I thought the demon might have left.

"…Here, kitty kitty."

Misty perked up and my heart stuck in my throat.

"Heeerrre, kitty kitty kitty."

She started toward the edge of my bed. I scrambled to grab any part of her. *"Misty! Misty, stay! Don't–"*

She slipped through my fingers and landed on the floor. I didn't dare chase after her as she sat down halfway to the closet's opening. Piqued interest made the tip of her tail twitch.

"That's a good kitty… Come to mommy…"

"Misty…! Misty! *Psh psh psh!*" I tried to coax her back. Only her tail twitched in response.

"Here, kitty kittyyy!"

Curiosity was too great of a temptation. She started

toward the closet. I couldn't look away when the front half of her body entered the shadows.

Mrow–

Something snatched her before she could finish uttering a mew of interest. I only saw it for a moment in the moonlight: a spindly hand of rotting flesh. Human fingers aren't supposed to be that long, nor nails that sharp.

The crunching. That awful crunching. I would have preferred to hear Misty screaming instead of the bone-crushing horror. It was the slurping that made me sick to my stomach. That wet, drawn-out suction of something torn and fleshy. I could never prepare myself for the anguish that sound would bring.

I knew then that I was right to be terrified. Nothing could have made me leave my bed. Whatever was in my closet was hungry, and would snatch whatever came within reach.

*   *   *

MY eyes refused to focus the next morning. Sleep never came for me, though perhaps insanity had. How much more could I take before it was too much?

"Misty…! Mistyyy!"

I could hear my mom calling our cat for breakfast. Should I tell her Misty wouldn't be running to her bowl of wet food this morning? I hadn't been able to look at my closet for more than a second, even in the daylight. Within that time, I saw tufts of cat hair on the ground before I refused to look any further. The door remained open. After what I saw, I wasn't going anywhere near it.

"*Pss pss pss! Here kitty!*" My mother tried time and time

again for a cat that wouldn't come.

Breakfast wasn't appetizing. I couldn't stand the thought of chewing, much less being in the same room as my mother. How could I when her face haunted me every night?

I went to school as a husk of my usual self. A math test went completely unanswered, leaving the teacher concerned. My responses were barely coherent when she pulled me aside after class. I suspect I might be in trouble when they contact my parents, but it didn't matter. It felt like a punishment when the bus left me at home. I didn't want to go back into that house.

As usual, Mom was busy in the kitchen when I walked in. She didn't seem to notice my quiet arrival and continued humming over a cutting board. I would have said hello, but I still harbored resentment from last night. Maybe if she had let me sleep on the couch, Misty's food bowl wouldn't have still been untouched.

I decided to return to my room only once. I would gather several necessities and clothes, then sleep somewhere else. I didn't care where, so long as it wasn't in the same room as that *thing*.

My room was cold upon my arrival. No part of it felt safe, even with the sun shining outside. I was determined not to look at the closet. Even from the corner of my eye, I could see it was still cracked open. That thing could have my room. I didn't care.

"*Caleb...*"

A whisper drifted out. I was hardly surprised, though I didn't expect it during the daylight.

"Shut up. I'm not listening," I said while throwing some clothes in a bag.

"*C... C-Caleb...!*"

I paused. This didn't sound like the ghoul; it sounded like a little girl terrified of being heard. I dared to look at the closet.

"Justine...?"

A tiny hand wrapped around the door before her head peeked into view. I had never seen such fear in her eyes.

"What's wrong? You look like–"

Her voice was barely audible. "I-I don't think that's mommy downstairs..."

To anyone else that statement would have sounded outlandish, but I knew what she meant. I knew right away.

Justine's eyes grew wide. The color drained from her face as she stared over my shoulder. I realized I had my back to the hallway and I started to wonder if it had been such a good idea to leave my door open.

Her voice dripped over my neck like decay.

"Caleb, when did you sneak past me? Welcome home, sweetie...! *Would you like a snack?*"

My limbs moved faster than ever before. I scrambled across my carpet into the closet, joining Justine. She was terrified. There was no time for me to be frightened; I had to be a big brother.

"Kids...?" our mother asked, stepping forward. A plate of after-school snacks sat in her hands like bait. They were messy and haphazard, nothing like the real thing. She couldn't fool me. "What's gotten into you two? You need to start on your homework!"

Justine started to bawl. I wrapped my arms around her in protection when our mother stepped closer and knelt down. We stared at her from within the curtain of my shirts. For all the fear this closet had given me over the past few nights, I had never expected it to become our refuge.

"Justine? What's wrong, baby? Why are you–"

"NO! *GET AWAY FROM HER!*"

I surprised myself with my scream. Our mother's eyes bulged in shock and she faltered. Several ants on a log slid from the plate and landed on my carpet.

"*YOU'RE NOT OUR MOM!*"

Justine's face was buried in my arm. I could feel tears soaking through my shirt. My shouts had to rise to maximum volume to make it over her cries. All the fear I'd had of this monster had turned to rage. I was tired of the torment.

Our mother's face sagged. Her gaze settled on my sister. "Justine… Baby, what happened? Have you been hiding in here this entire time?"

She nodded. "You're not my mommy! *I saw you!*"

"Saw me what, honey?" She came forward and reached a hand into the closet. I recoiled and she stopped short. Moisture made her eyes shine. "Kids, it's me!"

To see her feign such hurt only made me angrier. "Get away! *Get away from us!*"

Being the younger one and in such a frightened state, Justine was taking most of our mother's concern. She knelt down and opened her arms. "Come here, baby… I'm right here. What happened?"

Justine looked up and then away.

"Don't look at her," I warned.

"Caleb, shh. She's scared." She motioned once more. "Can I have a hug from my little girl? I want to tell her how much I love her!"

My sister looked up. Her crying faltered.

"I have a big, *BIG* hug for my baby! And kisses to make her feel all better!"

"Don't listen to–"

"*Caleb*," our mother hissed in warning. "Your sister is scared. I don't know what game you have been playing with her, but it has to stop. Let her go."

"But–"

She moved forward. "Come here, baby… You can help me make dinner before daddy gets home, ok?"

I couldn't stop her. Justine escaped my arms and ran from my closet into the arms of that monster. For how much fear she'd caused me, I was still powerless against her authority. Even if it was false.

"*Mwa mwa mwa mwa mwa!*" Exaggerated kisses assaulted Justine when my mother got ahold of her. Tears turned into giggles as every bit of fright melted away. She stood up with Justine in her arms and turned to leave my room.

"J-Justi–"

A final warning was thrown over my mother's shoulder. "Enough of this game, Caleb. Your sister hasn't slept in days. *Stop scaring her.*"

They left. I sat there, alone in my closet. Clothes hung around me and bunched on top of my head. I couldn't believe I had let her slip out of my arms so easily. Would Dad listen to me if I told him? Could I even get him alone before it was too late?

I shivered in my little hovel as I listened to them start cooking downstairs. The hangers clanked above me. What should I do? Where could I go? Could I sneak out my window and make it to a friend's house? Maybe their parents would listen and–

Something tickled the back of my neck. A cold layer of sweat broke out over my skin.

"Such a good boy… Protecting your sister…"

I bristled and froze.

"You knew right away that wasn't your real mother…"

I wanted to run. I tried to stand up, but a long, spindly hand had draped itself over my shoulder from behind my clothes. That voice of gurgling sludge dripped down my back. The closet felt like an icy abyss behind me. I wanted to cry out, to scream at my mother and sister so happily cooking dinner downstairs, but my voice was paralyzed.

The thing laughed in my ear and the hand tightened. *"Now come give your mother a hug."*

"MOMM–"

Air was ripped from my lungs and tore my words away. I was pulled back, deep, deep into the closet. The door raced a mile away as that hand yanked. My voice jumped from my throat too late. A squeak of fright barely escaped before the door slammed shut and swallowed my screams.

About *The Gap in the Closet*

This was the first story I wrote for this anthology. I can't say there's much originality to it; doppelgangers aren't new, and familial mimics trying to lure you to your doom aren't exactly groundbreaking horror elements. But lack of novelty doesn't make them any less gripping. In fact, I think that's why these uncanny horror elements are so common: they're effective.

Fear of the uncanny is hard-wired into our brains. Instincts tell us we need to be afraid of human faces that don't look quite right. That we need to be cautious and untrusting of the slightly off. Some theories explain the fear of the uncanny as our mind's way of protecting us from things like corpses and the disease they carry. I prefer one of the more outlandish theories: the fact that we have an evolutionary fear of the uncanny means that at some point in our distant past, there was some form of predator that mimicked its prey to hunt. Those who could tell the difference survived. Those who couldn't... Well, they found out what was really waiting in the darkness.

Rest in Peace

"AHH! GAHH!"

I jolted awake in a frantic scramble for air. Darkness held me in its grasp, as a frigid cold drilled its icy fingers into my bones. I couldn't see my own hand in front of my face. Everything was silent. I knew I was breathing, but the darkness was so thick, I couldn't even hear my own gasps for air. The back of my head flared with pain. I could still feel the rock that had hit me.

My fists and feet flung outward. I was allowed only inches before they struck wooden walls. Dull thuds responded to my strikes. It didn't take a genius to know I was underground.

I couldn't believe it at first. My breath came out in rising huffs before my anger exploded.

"You bastards! *YOU DAMN BASTARDS!*"

Spittle flew from my mouth with the curses. My lips were dry, cracking as I screamed below ground. I desperately needed water. They felt like they'd stretched over my teeth.

The coffin's lid rang against my elbow. I didn't care about the pain; they weren't going to get away with this. Specks of dirt fell through the lid's seam with every jolt. The soil was still loose: good news for me. Every strike was more earth moved.

"You   buried   me?   *ME?   YOU   GODDAMN*

BACKSTABBIN' SNAKES!* NOBODY DOES THIS TO DIAMONDBACK! *NOBODY!"* I loosed a rageful bellow into the surrounding earth. *"LET ME OUT!"*

There was nothing coming from above. No sounds. No movement. Not even the hoof falls from my trusty horse. The worms and bugs didn't even want to recognize me.

I pressed my hands to either side of the coffin. I had to when I felt like it was closing in around me. It was cheap, I could tell that much. It wouldn't be able to take much of a beating, especially with the weight of all that dirt on top.

My breath was weak, squeezed from my ribs by the tomb. How long had I been out? When did they get me? There wasn't an unlimited amount of air at my disposal. I was already feeling lightheaded.

I needed a tool. Something. Anything to help break the coffin.

My knees immediately struck the lid when I bent my legs. I had less room in here than a kid in a whore's belly.

"I'll get 'em… *I'll get 'em for this!"*

My shoulders ached when I stretched my arms along my body. They at least had the decency to leave my revolver, likely so I could end this imprisonment on my own terms. The next thing I noticed was the emptiness on my right hip.

The bag of gold dust and nuggets was gone. One of the biggest hauls of my life and it had been stolen while they tossed me into this early grave.

"YOU BASTARRRRDS!"

My anger was turning the coffin into an oven. Even the cold dirt couldn't deny me my rage.

"I showed you that vein! I trusted you! We had a *deal!"*

My knuckles cracked when I punched the lid. *"WE HAD A DEAL!"*

I started pushing with my arms and legs. The coffin strained around me, groaning at its joints. Dirt had begun streaming in above my head. It was soft and fresh, still moist from being thrown on top of me. It washed over my face but I coughed it out and kept thrashing. I was getting out of here.

Dirt fell in my eyes. I blinked, ignoring the discomfort. Anger was my painkiller. I'm sure I would hurt later, but there would be time for that after I put a bullet between each of their eyes.

The coffin complained from my forces. I was making headway.

I felt it jolt. The right wall bulged outward before snapping from the top. I could tell they'd nailed the lid shut. Several of the spikes had already pierced my fingers in the darkness like rusty rattlers. My breath came out like a bull's as I fumed.

"I'll get you sonsabitches for this! You hear me? YOU HEAR ME? Y'AIN'T GETTIN' AWAY FROM OL' DIAMONDBACK! I'LL SLIT YOUR THROATS WHILE YOU SLEEP!"

There was no way to know how deep I was buried. It could have been a foot of dirt on top of me, it could have been six. If they were smart, they would have made it ten.

My hand split against the lid.

"Go behind my back? Ain't even got the decency to put me down first?"

Freshly dug soil toppled around my neck. The gaps were widening. The lid had more give every time.

"If y'all so much as touched my horse, I'll skin you alive

before I *hang you!*"

I resorted to clawing at the edges of the splintering coffin. My nails gouged at the wood, shrieking in the darkness. It could have been blood running down my face, it could have been mud. All I knew was every scrape and every punch was one step closer to my vengeance.

My sore hands fumbled my revolver in the darkness. Pressing it against the wood, I gritted my teeth and pulled the trigger.

Silence.

My rage boiled. "*GRRRAHHHH!*"

I was going to wake the dead at this rate. They left my gun to end the torment on my own terms, and took out all the bullets.

"*Y'all're dead! DEAD!*"

My boot. I had to get to my boot. I couldn't lift my legs any higher than a few inches, but I could partially roll over and bend my legs toward me.

"*Nnngh!*"

I felt like my shoulder was going to dislocate itself from my straining. Finally, I felt the edge of the leather around my ankles. My fingers wiggled inside my boot to dig into a built-in pouch: my secret bullet stash. There were only six, but that was plenty.

Fumbling them into my revolver went by in an unseen blur. Several curses flew from my mouth when I dropped some and had to search in the darkness. I pressed the barrel against the top of the coffin, where I knew the most damage had been done.

All six rounds went off, but I only heard the first before

my hearing gave out. I couldn't even be certain I had heard any gunshot, as I flew into a desperate frenzy for escape. The bullets gently *thumped* around me, embedding themselves into the earth. Time below ground seemed to blur together. The concussive blasts made the wound in my head throb.

My fingers managed to hook into a gaping bullet hole. From there it was easy to start ripping the cheap wood apart. Dirt poured over me when my arm broke through. It tasted of rot and rainwater. Grit ground between my teeth when I spat the mouthfuls out, screaming into the gushing darkness. Even the earth wanted me to stay down.

The coffin was coming apart. I had broken through. If I kept my arms just right, I could keep myself from getting pinned beneath the dirt. It was pure luck that I had woken up before it had a chance to settle, or I might never have been able to move the lid.

"Nnggahhh! I'M COMIN' FOR YOU, YOU BASTARDS!"

My voice screamed through a mouth full of soil. I had managed to wriggle both arms out of the hole, pulling myself up through the dirt.

I was deep. Even with my arms straight up, pulling my torso out of the coffin, my fingers couldn't feel open air. It was a dance to keep the dirt moving around my body, exchanging it with my place in the coffin for the sake of mobility. The jagged edges on the lid pulled at my clothes as if the box wanted me to stay.

By the time I was sitting up, the dirt was crushing my ribs like a giant fist. I couldn't breathe. My arms had little leverage to pull my entire weight. I had to use my mouth to help claw my way up as if I were a worm.

My voice came out in dirt-gargling hisses. I could feel it

grating in the back of my sinuses. *"I'll kill y'all where you sleep! You and any whores y'all bought with my gold!"*

The earth moved easily around my hands. They had broken through to the surface, grasping at empty air. It was cold out, but not nearly as cold as that cursed coffin.

It was becoming easier now. I clawed at the surface and kicked myself from the coffin. Every inch was a blessing, delivering me like a demon from hell. The dirt started doming, lifted by my head and back. In a last-ditch effort to keep me prisoner, the coffin lid snagged my boot from below.

"GRRAHHHHH!"

My scream burst from the earth as I coughed. I inhaled like a newborn. The fresh air tasted better than any cigarette.

I grabbed at anything for a solid hold. The area around my grave was still firm and unforgiving. When my hips came above ground, I knew I had made it.

Dirt rolled off my back, and I crawled onto my hands and knees. A sinkhole was left in my wake from dirt entering my, would-be, resting place.

I had made it. Rage burned in my chest like a furnace. I was exhausted and aching. My head throbbed from where they had struck me. But I couldn't stop now. They had to pay.

The earth swayed beneath my legs when I rose. Dirt fell off my shoulders in curtains as I breathed deeply.

"Where are you?" I bellowed. "WHERE ARE YOU? I'M COMIN' FOR YOU, *YOU SONSABIT–"*

I paused, taking in my surroundings. It was night. Last I could remember, it was noon without a cloud in the sky. I held my hand up to block the moon's glow; even its silvery presence hurt after the darkness below.

"Wait…"

Why could I see the moon through my hand?

I brought my arm down, my eyes drifting over its thin form before catching sight of the rest of my body.

Bones… Just bones… I stood for a moment in contemplation, staring at my own skeleton. Realization made me stumble backward like a drunk.

"Oh… Right…"

My clothes hung off me in a tattered cover. There was no skin to block my skeleton from the moon. I thought I could hear the wind whistling through my ribs. My entire body sounded like a hollow wooden windchime as I moved. Clenching my hands open and closed, I stared at them with rising melancholy. My fingers were scratched and worn down. Some were completely broken in half. My entire right foot was gone, abandoned back in the coffin after the lid snagged my boot.

I rubbed the back of my skull. The hole was still there and as painful as ever.

"How long has it been this time…"

My surroundings drew my attention. There were more headstones every time I emerged. The town was still in the distance, glowing at the base of a hill. It was always larger than I remembered. Although now, I was left wondering how they managed to light it up so well at night. Never seen lanterns so bright and steady.

My jaw slacked with a sigh. My gold was long gone, same with those double-crossing snakes who took it. Maybe they're even buried in this same cemetery. I never get around to looking.

"I always forget…"

I clenched my hands in frustration, angry again at my

inability to stay dead.

"Damn hard to forgive an' forget..."

My body swayed in the breeze, uneasy on my aching bones. It was getting hard to stay upright and I was feeling tired as my anger ebbed.

Joints creaked when I stumbled back. A headstone provided support. My headstone. Always there... Always sturdy. I lowered to the ground. The smoothed rock was firm against my spine, solid and unmoving. My most trusted companion.

I rolled my head to the side, having forgotten what it said. The inscription was faded but not illegible.

"1847, huh... Wonder what year it is now..."

The other headstones could have given me a clue, but it wasn't worth the effort. My hand scooped some of the loose dirt from my grave. Based on the shovel nearby, they must have reburied me only a day or two ago.

This vengeance won't let me sleep.

I leaned back and lifted my empty sockets toward the sky. A bright moon hung there, weightless as always.

"At least you never change. No matter how many times I claw myself out..."

The world was slipping away. It never failed, once everything came rushing back. Slumping against my own headstone, I could feel that eternal sleep taking over. My vision darkened and my bones settled.

"Guess I'll just wait here... Someone'll put me back..."

I stared at the shovel stuck in the ground by my headstone as the world faded.

"Someone always does..."

<u>About *Rest in Peace*</u>

At first, Rest in Peace *was meant to be a simple story about being buried alive. It's one of the more common fears and I wanted to tap into that. As I got into writing it, though, I realized there wasn't an ending I found satisfying.*

It got me wondering what it's like to be locked in a coffin six feet underground. Assuming you're not there against your will, I imagine it's quiet, cold, and dare I say, peaceful. After all, we say 'rest in peace'. But what if that rest isn't peaceful? In fact, what if that rest is downright dripping in vengeance? What could keep someone from that peaceful sleep? Exploring those questions led me to the ending I wanted, and I hope it was a surprise.

Don't let yourself be like Diamondback. He's so full of hatred and wrath that even death can't keep him quiet. There is so much noise in the world designed to keep us awake at night and tossing and turning in bed. Don't give it the satisfaction of robbing you of your peace. If it's doing that, chances are, it's already robbed you of enough throughout the day. You deserve to rest in peace

Safe
Haven

I'VE always enjoyed traveling for work. It's different from a normal road trip. There's a distinct purpose to it. A goal. A reason why you're journeying across the land. It's not for fun. It's a quest of sorts entrusted to you by the higher-ups. But in this quest, there's something deeper, where I've found a level of melancholy tranquility: the hotel.

In travels to lands of unfamiliarity, you always manage to find a bed. Somewhere to sleep. The outside world simply fades away when I close that door. I'm in my own little bubble of comfort. A place separated from the journey. It doesn't matter how alien the environment might be; within those walls, everything is familiar. A bed… a tv… a shower… maybe some pizza… The hotel is a slice of consistency. A safe haven of the known, keeping the endless unknown at bay. I've always thought it romantic, if not a little corny, and today was no exception.

The sun was nearing the horizon. There was roughly an hour left before dark, and I was enjoying everything the golden hour had to offer in the middle of open country. A day of driving had left me in a part of eastern Washington with more farm fields than trees. In the setting sun, they all glowed orange. I would have continued driving, if I hadn't seen the sign for a small town by the name of Lind.

The town wasn't big. Someone more in shape could probably run around the entire thing once or twice and call it a modest workout. I didn't even need the GPS to help me get to the hotel; I could pick it out simply by looking down the road: *The Motor Inn.*

It was a small roadside motel. My company didn't like splurging on the fancy three or four-star stays. These small rinky-dink places saved them a couple bucks. I didn't mind at the end of the day; the smaller hotels felt homier. More cozy.

I claimed one of the few remaining parking spots as my own. The hotel itself consisted of two floors built into a horseshoe shape opening toward Lind's main road. The late '60s still clung to the exterior like a sticky residue you could never quite remove. Chances were, the rooms had been updated since then, but I wouldn't know until flicking on the light.

My ears took a moment to adjust to the absence of my music when I turned the car off. Outside, the June air was warm and smelled of country freshness. The area was surprisingly lively for its size. Across the street were a dozen kids playing baseball. A significant portion of the parking lot was devoted to a Coffee Hut. Even this late at night, it had a handful of cars waiting in line. Some guests were sprinkled through the inn's parking lot, either on their way to their rooms or just shooting the breeze. A few blocks away, it sounded like a family was enjoying an eventful birthday party.

I would take this over a four-star hotel in a busy city any day.

A rotating fan circulated the air of the main office. Years of cigarette smoke had stained the walls yellow. Magazines and a dirty coffee pot populated a makeshift sitting area. Behind the front desk was a larger woman, too bored for her own good. A TV with bunny ears was blaring some game show, for her viewing pleasure only. The Price is Right, by the sounds of it. Next to her mess of papers, sat a cat bed and one feline enjoying a nap before an evening prowl.

An annoyed glance flashed over a pair of thick orange glasses. "Checkin' in?"

"Yea, should be under–"

She cleared her throat of a juicy nugget. "Last name?"

"Blythe."

The Price is Right stole a dozen seconds more of her attention before she started looking through her book. "Credit card to keep on file?" There was a momentary scowl when she saw the picture on my personalized card but nothing was said. I was surprised at how warm the plastic was when she handed it back. "Any pets?"

"Nope."

"Sign here."

She slid an agreement and pen across the counter with hardly a look away from the TV. A quick scribble, and I returned the sheet. Her cat tensed into a long-legged stretch and yawned. Compared to the lively sounds of traffic and children playing across the street, the check-in desk was a morgue.

"Do you want a pillow?"

I blinked, unsure if I'd heard correctly. "Excuse me?"

Repeating herself seemed to be a major inconvenience. "Pillow? For the bed?"

"Oh… Yes, please…?"

"Here." A white rectangle blob with faint stains was withdrawn from behind the counter. I watched her struggle to put on a pillowcase without looking away from the TV. "You're in room 214. No loud noises after nine. Donuts are set out at six. Checkout is ten. If you need anything, I'm here until ten tonight."

I was surprised to see a set of keys tossed on the counter rather than a keycard. All hopes of an updated interior were dashed. Taking my room's access, I gave a last friendly smile. "Have a good one!"

"Mhm," the receptionist grunted.

She couldn't have picked me out from a lineup if I came back to rob the register five minutes later; the price must have been *very* right tonight.

It was cleansing to step back into the outside world, and breathe air that didn't smell like cigarettes and cat litter. Given the state of the motel, I was surprised by its popularity. I could hardly see an empty parking space as I made my way to the stairs and up to the second floor. Across the road, I watched one kid kick up a cloud of dust as he sprinted around the baseball diamond.

"Evenin'," an aged man greeted when I walked past. A rusty metal chair sat outside his room next to a small beer cooler. By the looks of things, he was already two cans deep. A coffee can of cigarette butts told me this wasn't his first or second night at the motel.

I nodded and took care not to strike his foot with my suitcase and cooler. "Fine one at that."

There came a solemn nod of agreement before he tilted his head back and finished his third can.

My room was another door down. Passing 213, I could hear the muffled sound of a TV with the volume turned high enough to drown out any form of conversation. The person inside was either old, near-deaf, dead, or a combination of all three. I tried to tell myself it wouldn't be so bad through the walls, but deep down I knew there was no such hope.

The TV was only louder when I opened my room to a musty darkness. Action and screaming dialogue came through the drywall, distorted and muffled like an old dream. I leaned back outside and watched their blinded window flash with the TV's content. A brief urge to knock on 213's door came and went with a meditative breath; there was a chance they would turn it off while I got settled. At least my other neighbor's room was dark. It was vacant compared to the cinephile next door.

Putting the TV out of my mind, I returned to my own accommodations for the night. They weren't completely outdated, but nothing about them had changed in the last ten or twenty years. The bed cover's design reeked of the early '90s and the carpet was a dark green draped in gold waves. A boxy TV took up the majority of a dresser that sat next to a barebones work desk. On the far side of the room was a sink and a door to a bathroom. Its blue-tiled walls and yellow shower-tub combo fitted into the wall felt decades out of place. You certainly get what you pay for.

Despite the age, it did feel clean and I could sense that familiar bubble of solitude around me. This room might not have been much, but it was *my* safe haven for the night, while this rambunctious little town whirred on.

I took in the room for a moment before I decided on my next steps. There was no rush to start the night; I wanted to take a play from my neighbor's book and watch the sunset. A few minutes later after a little unpacking, I was descending the steps into the parking lot. I was just in time to get to the Coffee Hut as the last car drove off from the line. A younger girl, likely still in high school, greeted me within the tiny structure.

"Can I get ya anything?" she asked with bubbly enthusiasm.

"Just a decaf coffee, please."

It was oddly pleasant waiting for my drink. I could have waited in the setting sun for hours and been content taking in the life around me. Every little detail this town had to offer was worth enjoying. It wasn't often you saw kids playing baseball like this anymore. There was a nostalgic atmosphere to it. One boy vanished into a dust storm when he slid home. There was a tiny uproar when he was deemed out.

"Two dollars, please!"

I paid with a five and told her to keep the change. There would be just enough time to sip my decaf and enjoy the afternoon air before the sun set for good.

The metal railing outside my room was pleasant to lean on. Warm comfort soaked through my core, as I drank my coffee. In the distance, the highway snaked through the desolate countryside with halves of white and red. Hard to believe it was so busy this time of day, like some sort of perpetual rush hour. Down the corridor the old man hadn't moved, now nursing beer number four.

I raised my cup and nodded before joking, "Let me know if you need some help hiding those!"

A grin missing several teeth flashed back. From across the open lot he agreed, "Never mind some company. I'll be out here for another hour or two if that's a real offer."

In truth, it hadn't been an actual desire but a friendly musing. Enjoying the night air with beer, pizza, and some conversation didn't sound bad, though.

"I just might join ya. Give me a bit."

I looked around as the last of my coffee trickled away. The air had adopted a gentle breeze. There was an absence I couldn't place. I looked across the road. The baseball game had ended. The kids were gone. I must have been lost in thought more than I realized, because I couldn't see any of them walking home in any direction. The only sign there had been anyone playing at all was a lone bat abandoned near home plate.

It would have been peaceful bliss if my neighbor's TV wasn't blaring like a siren. I wasn't ready to face the noise or lodge a complaint. It would be quiet hours soon enough and the problem would either resolve itself, or I would have grounds to complain.

I decided a walk was in order. Stretch my legs after a day of driving, before I truly enter relaxation mode for the night. Feeling thoughtful, I left the motel's property for a few minutes of exploration. A neighborhood opened up just a block over with an old self-serve car wash at the corner. Its streets were wide and the yards were enclosed with a chest-high chain link fence. Concrete had spiderwebbed into a mess of cracks and missing chunks. The neighborhood was likely a few decades older than the motel. These were cookie-cutter WWII houses with more weeds than grass.

I strode down several sidewalks, taking in the scenery. I expected to see some of the baseball kids running around or to send a few dogs into a protective fit, but there was only silence.

Nothing.

Unease scratched at the back of my mind. Out of common courtesy, I'd been avoiding doing so but I now turned my attention higher and deliberately looked into the windows of passing houses.

They were all empty. Some were dark, some had lights

on inside revealing a kitchen or living room, but all were devoid of life. I asked myself if I had seen a single person since I started my walk. None came to mind, but who keeps track of every person they pass by or see out of the corner of their vision? There was the party I'd heard earlier from several blocks away, but now there wasn't a trace.

Cars were in the driveways. Toys peppered some yards. I paused at a corner and looked down all four streets. Not a sign of life looked back. I couldn't even recall seeing a single car drive by.

I shivered at the thought of what felt like a deserted ghost town. The coffee's warmth was wearing off and the sun was all but below the horizon.

My feet turned around before I'd told them to. I was sure everyone was just busy. Maybe there was a community event tonight. A football game at the school. Something the entire neighborhood could attend without their cars…

Strange how walking alone can leave you feeling the most followed when your mind starts to wander.

Returning to The Motor Inn brought a sigh of relief. My haven was still here. Quieter than before, but still here. Mr. Beer gave a content wave when I unlocked my room. Whatever unease I had vanished when I closed that door behind me and the world outside my bubble vanished along with it.

I dialed the number for a pizza joint recommended by a pamphlet on the desk. Despite the neighbor's TV drowning out my words, I managed to place an order: one large pepperoni guaranteed in thirty minutes or less. Just enough time to shower and settle in, while I debated joining the old stranger for a beer or two.

No sooner than turning on the water had I noticed the

absence of towels. I almost felt stupid for assuming they would be there. If pillows weren't a given, why would such a luxury as towels be?

I headed for the front desk with some speed in my step. Maybe I could mention the overbearing TV volume while I was there.

The door was open and the light was on, but the old woman had left her post. An episode of Jeopardy had taken the place of The Price is Right.

Mrooowwlll…!

The cat greeted me and rolled in its bed. I dared to give its belly a scratch before tapping the reception bell. Its ringing cut through the office and into the dimming evening outside. Seconds turned into minutes. She wasn't in the restroom; I could see the door open and the light off.

"Hello?"

Nothing but purring. I couldn't stay forever. Pizza waits for no man, and I had to shower. A glance behind the counter presented me with stacks of towels. I grabbed two and headed for the door.

"Tell her 214 took them!" I told the cat.

I took a shortcut through the parking lot back to the stairs with my boon. My steps felt like they reverberated through the entire structure but I wanted to hurry.

The door was almost closed behind me when I paused. Unease had returned. I stood with my back to the walkway before turning around and looking out over the parking lot below.

It had been packed with cars only thirty minutes ago. Now it was half empty. I hadn't even noticed while I was running through. When had they left? All while I was taking my walk? In that short amount of time? I had been outside otherwise. I wanted to tell myself I would have noticed them driving away. My attention attained greater focus as the unease grew.

The Coffee Hut was gone. I could see the outline on the pavement created from years of sitting in one place. Surely the owner must have just taken it home. Maybe it roams the town. It definitely had a tongue on the front for towing. Someone could hook up and go in a few minutes. I could picture it so clearly in my mind. But if it was mobile, why was the outline square with no wheels?

I noticed I was clutching the towels tighter. The air was still and calm. Something was missing… Unease teased my throat when I realized it was the distant mechanical roar of the highway. I could just make it out in the dusk-embraced distance. The road was gray, but the red and white snakes of light were gone.

A moment of internal panic passed. I was tired. Hungry. Exhausted after a long day of driving. Any unease I was feeling was only in my head. There's no reason the parking lot's vacancy couldn't fluctuate; cars come and go. And coffee shacks were meant to be mobile. Even highways saw momentary downturns. Had I stood there for a few more seconds, I was certain I would have seen some headlights return.

But I shook it from my mind. Not because I was frightened of the seconds turning into minutes, but because I knew it was ridiculous. I made a mental face of amusement at myself and turned back toward my room.

I wish I had turned the other way to leave.

Mr. Beer was gone. Along with his rusty chair. Three empty cans remained, along with his cooler of unopened drinks.

My door slammed harder than it should have after that. I leaned against it and felt my heart racing. I couldn't explain why the old man's scarcity had been the thing to shake me to my core. The other things I could rationalize, but him… He was a constant. Even if I'd known him for less than an hour, I knew he was supposed to be sitting out there.

The shower wasn't as calming as it should have been. My mind couldn't shake the feeling of something being out of place. Something missing. My safe haven wasn't meant to feel this secluded. Deep down I knew there was nothing wrong: cars come and go. Neighborhoods quiet down. Receptionists couldn't be at their desks 24/7. People couldn't sit in the walkway drinking beers all night.

Even still… None of it sat right. My shower wouldn't have been relaxing regardless of the strange happenings; the neighbor's TV was blaring over the rush of my old pipes and shower head. I think the tiled walls only made the sounds bounce around more.

Forty-five minutes had passed by the time I stepped out. A headache was creeping upon me as I stared at the digital clock and fought against the pounding TV volume coming through the wall and into my head. Frustration felt ready to boil over with my hunger. I was ready to take my anger out on whichever poor high schooler picked up at the pizza place, then I could go to the office and tell them about the loud TV.

I redialed the pizza shop. The phone paused before giving a trio of ascending beeps.

We're sorry, but your call cannot be completed as dialed. Please hang up and try again.

I'd dialed it wrong. I must have. Looking between the pamphlet and keypad, I called once more. Another pause.

We're sorry, but your call cannot be completed as dialed. Please hang up and try again.

My thumb turned white when I ended the call with a forceful button press. Those three beeps rang in my head like a bell as I entered the pizza place's number a third time, double-checking each digit. The phone's plastic creaked under my thumb with every angry press.

A pause.

We're sorry, but your call cannot be completed–

"What the hell?"

I think I was hoping the neighbor heard me slam the phone back on its receiver and register a hint at my frustration from his TV. The clock told me it had been an hour since I ordered my dinner. Somehow, I didn't think it would be coming.

What better time for a trip to the front desk and to grab some ice for a drink. I longed for the pensive romance the evening had provided an hour ago when I left my room. Now I was just hungry and annoyed. I sent a glare at room 213 on my way to the stairs and cursed them under my breath.

There was a wind pulling the air like a giant vacuum was pulling on the atmosphere from out of sight. It smelled stale and dry, as if the area hadn't seen moisture in weeks. The absence of the highway's raucous was almost louder than the traffic would have been if it wasn't still deserted.

A room across the parking lot sat open. The door was slamming against the deadbolt in the wind, hard enough to send guttural thuds throughout the complex. Maybe their pizza was missing too. I tried ignoring the fact that my car was one of only three in the entire lot. There must have been some kind of event going on tonight.

I walked into the front office with my complaint loaded on my tongue.

"Can you please tell the people in 213 to turn their–"

The front desk was empty. There was no grumpy old woman. No game show playing on the television; there wasn't even a television. I spied no sleepy cat nor its fur-covered bed. The desk was as bare as could be.

I couldn't deny my discomfort now. My heart was racing by the time I speed-walked back to my room and locked the door. I realized I had forgotten my ice, but I didn't care. You couldn't make me go back outside at this point. Something unnatural was going on. The air wasn't right. It didn't sit in my lungs properly.

I fished a can of warm beer out of my iceless cooler and drank half in one go while my head throbbed against the neighbor's TV. Most likely, I was being irrational. Whatever was happening had a sound explanation. I was simply tired from driving so far. Tired and hungry. Any minute now my pizza would show up.

THUD!

THUD!

Someone's at the door. The relief I felt in that moment was immeasurable. I set my beer on the nightstand and approached the door to accept my late delivery. They certainly wouldn't be getting a tip.

The doorway was empty upon opening. I looked left and right down the walkway, and saw no one in the eerie darkness.

THUD!

THUD THUD!

THUD!

THUD!

I turned toward the neighbor's wall. There was a rhythmic, rapid pounding, mixed with a woman's moans. They were having sex next door. Energetic enough to make the frames on my wall bounce with every strike of their headboard.

THUD!

THUD!

THUD!

My temples throbbed as I sat on the edge of my bed trying to endure the noise. It all built into a monstrous tempo: their bed, their TV, the wind beating on the windows and door. Everything. There was too much.

THUD!

THUD THUD!

It was too much. I couldn't take it. I ran at the wall and beat my fist against its echoing surface.

"HEY KNOCK IT *OFF!*"

THUD!

THUD!

THUD!

I pounded again and felt my voice grow hoarse at my yelling. *"TURN IT DOWN!"*

They were too busy to hear me, or happy to ignore my complaint.

THUD!

THUD!

The edge of my bed greeted me, and I drank the rest of my beer before flipping on my own TV. It glowed to life, and I cranked the volume as high as it could go in retaliation. Together our speakers filled the atmosphere with indecipherable noise, broken only by their bed and a woman on the verge of ecstasy.

THUD!

THUD!

I wanted to scream. My fingers massaged my temples against the chaos. Closing my eyes made it seem like a freakish sensory nightmare.

"Turn it off... Please, just turn it offffff..."

THUD!

THUD!

THU–

It stopped. Their TV died. The pounding ceased. I looked up from my hands and stared with unease at their wall, as my TV filled my room with a dialog between two cops.

The sounds had stopped, but not in a natural way. They'd cut off abruptly. My ears ached, as if waiting for a natural fade out. The sounds had simply died halfway through. Unfinished.

SSHHHHHHHH!

I yelped when my TV cut to a screen of static. Flashing filled my room. White noise blared loud enough to hurt my ears. The remote fumbled in my hand before I turned it off in a panic.

It was absolutely silent then. I could hear myself think. I could hear myself breathe. My heartbeat in my ears.

This was too quiet now. The world wasn't supposed to be this quiet.

I turned my TV back on and rapidly brought the volume down before flipping through the channels hoping to find the news.

Everything was snow. I went through the channel list three times before I gave up. Even then, I couldn't bear to turn the television off. I needed some kind of noise, even if it was static. I almost wished the couple next door would start back up again.

It had become bright outside. Light streamed through the gap between the blackout curtains. The street lights must have finally come on and were pointing directly at my window.

I sat for a time, wondering what to do. It was still early, but my mind refused to think. My safe haven wasn't as pleasant this time around. I felt more trapped than peaceful. One beer had been more than enough to give me a buzz. Not surprising when I had nothing in my belly. Wherever my pizza had ended up, I hoped someone was enjoying it.

Eventually, after what felt like an hour of staring at the wall, I decided to sleep. White noise, on the lowest volume, shielded me against the unnatural silence of the outside. It still wasn't enough to keep every creak from my bed from cutting through the night like a knife.

*   *   *

THE white noise was still going when I awoke to my alarm at six. There was a lot of driving to do, and an early start with some coffee and donuts was just the way to kick it off. Last night's stress was gone. Sleep had defeated my hunger as well as the raging headache. A donut would kickstart my appetite, and some lucky sandwich would have the pleasure of meeting my stomach in a few hours for a well-deserved lunch.

A quick swish of water was enough to clear the sleep from my mouth. I elected to brush my teeth and freshen up after having the sugary pastry. Throwing on a shirt, I grabbed my red coffee mug and headed for the door.

Outside was white. Everything. Blinding white. At first, I thought it had somehow snowed several feet in the summer, but there was truly nothing. There was no depth. No concrete walkway. No railing. No parking lot. No road, hotel, or highway. The world stopped at the edge of my threshold and fell into a white abyss.

I stared out into nothingness for several minutes. A few times I closed the door and reopened it expecting the outside to reappear. But there was always nothing. Less than nothing. My eyes couldn't even focus on it. It hurt to look at.

No sounds came from the abyss. No wind. No signs of life. My voice didn't carry more than what sounded like a foot outside my door. How could it? There was nothing for the sound to bounce off.

Questions of sanity clawed at my mind. I lifted one leg out of the door and over into the void in preparation to take a step. Just because I couldn't see it didn't mean there was nothing there. With more confidence than was wise, I shifted my balance and leaned onto my waiting foot.

My heart jumped out of my chest when my foot fell beyond the threshold and plunged into nothingness. I grappled with the doorframe to keep myself inside. Sweat appeared on my body in a flash as I realized how close I'd come to walking into nothing. A scrape ran up the back of my leg where it had been scratched along the bottom of the door frame.

Surely, I had to be dreaming. Any excuse to keep the panicked confusion at bay.

I inspected it deeper. Leaning out as far as I dared, I could see the outer corner of my room formed by the building. The brick was still there creating the wall. Getting on my stomach, I inched my way to the edge and craned my head under my threshold. There was only smooth concrete beneath my room. No supports. No marks. Nothing but emptiness.

I stayed like that for some time, surprisingly calm given

the circumstances. Maybe it was too much for my brain to truly process into fear. Still on my stomach, I reached for my coffee mug and held it over the edge. My hand hovered there with indecision until it shook with fatigue.

The mug fell. I watched it, never blinking. Its sharp red color was like a drop of blood on a piece of paper. It shrunk as it fell silently into the void. I watched until the little red speck vanished from my sight. There was never a crash. No shattering.

Nothing.

Panic took me like the jaws of a lunging tiger. I slammed the door shut and scrambled backward on all fours until my back collided with the bed. TV static buzzed in my ears while I wrestled with whatever hell I had found myself in. I didn't dare move for fear of the floor falling out from under me. I only sat there, staring at the flawless white nothingness filling my window.

It was creeping in. The solitude. The mind-numbing silence. The ever-stretching stillness of complete oblivion. I was already starting to hear things. Distant voices, too large for any one living organism. How long until I followed my coffee mug into the void? Maybe death had vanished along with everything else in the world. Already, I found myself wondering about that path of no return. Would I prefer a life of eternity in this room, or an eternity of falling through nothing?

Denial stole my breath as I pushed the inevitable choice out of my mind.

For now, this room was everything. All that remained. This room was my world. My universe. I could stay here for as long as my sanity allowed. It was my one protection against that endless forever. I had no choice but to embrace it for however long my sanity deemed fit.

My safe haven.

About _Safe Haven_

I poured a lot of myself into this one. At least the parts before things start going 'poof'. Hotels are one of the most romantic places out there, and I mean that in a literary sense. Don't worry, I won't ramble on about my feelings on them again. I've already done that for several pages here. I find solace in the idea that out of the entire world and your travels for the day, you've come to find a single, specific spot on Earth where you can call home for the night.

This particular story was based on a motel I stayed at, while my wife and I were traveling to watch my sister's half-marathon race in Coeur d'Alene, Idaho. It was the Gateway Inn, located in Grangeville, Idaho. We took a walk around the area at dusk before ordering pizza and settling in for the night. The highway wound far into the horizon in the background... The neighborhood was quiet... Everything was the same, but different. It's not a feeling we're gifted with often. That setting didn't exist before you stopped there, and unless you frequent the area, chances are it stopped existing for you the moment you drove off.

That's what hotels are for. Yes, they let you rest, but they also give you permission to poke around a different world for a little bit before passing through.

Patchwork

A desolate countryside flew by. What wasn't pavement, was pastures and fields of corn browning with the onset of fall. Ahead of James and Angel, was a sky painted with the colors of dusk. Striking oranges, reds, and purples lined the horizon in a gradient of approaching darkness. It would have been a beautiful sight if the atmosphere wasn't so tense.

Angel had been quiet most of the drive but that wasn't new. Even after a few months, things haven't been the same. James wasn't sure they could ever be. He'd hoped a summer road trip would help, but he had to admit, thus far, it was lacking.

Tragedy couldn't always be swayed so easily.

"I thought you said the hotel was close." Angel's voice was short and annoyed. She'd been staring at the passing road for too long.

"It is!" Glancing at the odometer made James question his certainty. "Or it was supposed to be..."

A sign approached, half covered by the brown stalks. Faded paint advertised an old antiques and curio shop less than a mile away.

James smirked at the sign. "Silvia's Antiquities and Patchwork... Heh, need a dusty vase from the '40s? Maybe a creepy old doll?"

Angel's face soured and he knew he'd overstepped. A sigh thickened the atmosphere. "Just stop there and ask for directions. I'm tired."

They were at the shop in less than a minute. It stood over a surrounding cornfield with splintering weather-beaten wood. Paint had long abandoned the exterior to the elements. The first floor was plastered in signs and display windows while the second was dark. Stuck in the middle of nowhere, the building was an eyesore against the serene countryside. A surrounding dirt lot was eerily empty despite an open sign in the window.

James snorted. "Wow… Place must really be packed on the weekends."

Angel ignored him and slammed her car door to approach the structure. Some days were better than others. To see her long bright skirt fluttering so carefree in the wind was counterintuitive to her mood.

It was darker inside than James anticipated. Shelf upon shelf filled aisles of wares. Oddities and antiques assaulted the senses from all directions. Dust rose in clouds to swirl in the sun's setting rays, filtering through a drawn shade. The store was split in half, one side containing wares from various decades, while another featured a rustic tailor's workshop. Neither looked to host an impressive number of visitors. James noted spiderwebs stretching between various sewing supplies.

"Less of a curio shop and more of a pack rat's den…" James reached out to inspect a blue bracelet on a ragged porcelain doll. Its arm fell off with a delicate *clink*, causing him to panic and hide it on the shelf. "*You didn't see that,*" he whispered.

Angel didn't care to respond.

"Hello?" James's voice carried. At the back, he could see a flight of stairs. A rope blocked them with a sign reading: *Do*

Not Enter. "Maybe the owner lives upstairs… I didn't see another car here. Could be their house and shop."

His wife cast an uninterested glance. "Let's just go. Town can't be too far away from this dump. All this junk is a waste of time and I'm hungry."

"Oh it's not junk, my dear! Far from it!"

Both of them jumped at a scratchy voice. It was an old woman, decrepit and gnarbled with age. The top of her graying head reached no higher than James's chest. Nothing more than skin and bones, the leather apron around her neck looked too heavy for her to manage.

Weary, sunken eyes wavered between the two of them before settling on Angel. "What is it you're looking for, dear…?"

James interjected, "We were just trying to get to the next town. If you could–"

The old woman's eyes remained on Angel. They shined with understanding. Her smile melted into a gentle frown. "Oh… You're not searching for something… You're yearning… Yearning for something lost…"

Angel shifted her feet uncomfortably. She and James exchanged glances. "L-Listen, we–"

A wrinkled hand extended to place itself on Angel's stomach. "Something lost, and precious… Am I right, dear?"

Disbelief covered James's face. A random elderly woman could never have known about the miscarriage. Anxiety bubbled in his gut as he watched his wife tense under the woman's palm, remaining motionless. He asked again, "Can you please just tell us–"

Angel interrupted, nodding and answering the woman. "Y-Yes…" Her words cracked. *"That's right…"*

There was sorrow in her voice. A high-pitched mournful tone that James knew well by now. Moisture glistened in her eyes and James knew he had to stop talking.

The woman's hand pressed harder. "Oh yes... Something very precious... There's no pain quite like it, is there?" Scars ran along the length of her fingers and curled around her knuckles. Eyes sharp, she looked up at James and Angel. "What would you give to have it back?"

James stayed as silent as a rock. He watched his wife's mouth tremble at the question he already knew the answer to. There was a strange expression on Angel's face, one of dreamy grief-wrapped desire. He might have thought a genie was tempting her with a wish.

"A-Anything... *Anything...*" Angel's breath started to hitch. Tears were flowing. With the old woman's prodding, James was surprised Angel hadn't broken down into a sobbing heap. "*Anything to have her back...*"

A sweet smile wrinkled the woman's cheeks at Angel's answer. She removed her hand. "Not to worry, dear... A family is like a beautiful tapestry. Sometimes it's torn, but it's nothing a few stitches can't fix."

Angel's face softened. Outside, the sun set and threw the shop into malevolent shades of crimson. Shadows of waving corn stalks jumped from the floor to cast themselves over the woman, darkening her grin into something sinister. Shifting contours over her bones made James shiver. Her face looked closer to melted candle wax than aged skin.

The room continued to darken, far quicker than what was natural. A black fog crept around them. Before long, James realized it wasn't the world that was darkening; it was his vision.

"J… James…"

Angel slumped before collapsing at his side. *"H-Hey! Hey! Angel! What…"* He reached for her but his own balance was failing. The room spun. Antiques blurred into chaos. Woozy and disoriented, James fell to the floor next to his wife. A distant cackle echoed through his mind before consciousness abandoned him altogether.

*   *   *

THE world was dark and musty when James opened his eyes. Everything ached. His vision refused to focus, delivering only a blurred view of his surroundings. Rough floorboards scraped against his back as he rolled and groaned. Coughing felt like a hammer pounding against his ribs from within. Plumes of dust attacked his lungs. A flickering oil lantern served as the room's only illumination.

"A… Angel…?"

Distant mumbling drifted into his ears. He wasn't alone. Someone was nearby and working. Hesitant, he tried to sit up.

Pain erupted across his body. Head on fire, he placed one hand against his eye where it throbbed the most. Confusion wracked his mind when his vision remained unchanged. When he pulled his palm away, a layer of fresh blood coated his hand.

Panic rose into a geyser. His right eye wouldn't open. Trying to do so brought sharp discomfort. His fingertips brushed across tense ridges and points running along the seams of his eyelid.

It was sewn shut. Far worse, as he tenderly inspected the

socket, was the lack of pressure behind the thin layer of skin. It was empty. Hollow. Blood caked one side of his face where it had run free while he was unconscious. Even if he could open his eyelid, there was nothing left behind it to see.

Fear rampaged through him now. The preoccupied mumbles were louder and accompanied by soft cackles of amusement, like someone focusing hard on their work and enjoying every bit. James's breath quickened as he inspected the rest of his body.

His shirt was torn down the middle to expose a gruesome suture at the center of his sternum. The seam of skin was raw and purple after being so hastily sewn together. A chunk of muscle was missing from his leg as if a monster had taken a bite. Flesh was sewn over the cavity but did little to hide the gore. A total of three fingers were missing, reduced to throbbing stumps at the first knuckle.

Adrenaline flowed through his veins. Everywhere he looked, there were missing parts. Panic numbed the pain as he stood on weak legs. Stitches wanted to pop at his chest with every inhale.

The room was a horde of sewing supplies and random tools. Rusted needles and coils of thread hung from the ceiling, as if their owner might need them at a moment's notice. Everything from scissors, to hedge shears, to axes filled shelves and tables. Suspiciously thick pale bundles of leather sat piled high in a puddle of grime off to the corner.

However, one sight made James ignore everything else. Against one wall, wavered the shadow of something that cast dread into his soul.

"Hah... Almost there, dear... Don't you worry..."

The murmuring chilled his blood. James turned his head toward the source of the shadow despite every instinct telling him to run.

It was tall. A naked, gangly body of a malnourished elderly woman with stilt-like arms and legs, twice as long as they should have been, casting demonic shadows over the walls. An extra pair of limbs gave the hag a total of four hands. Wheezing breath brought its back to rise and fall. Lantern light played over the protruding ridges of its spine that ran from a balding head to its hips. Some parts of its body had been used as a fleshy pin cushion. Patches of skin held spare needles and scissors, each piece of metal jolting with every flex of its slender muscles. Decaying gray hair fell around its face as it straddled and hunched over the supine form of a woman. Needle-like fingers worked in a blur of deft movement over her exposed abdomen. Even at a distance, James could see the creature was suturing a massive laceration running vertically up Angel's stomach.

His voice was little more than a rasp. *"A-Angel?"*

The thing's head whipped toward his voice. A sneer revealed rancid gums and teeth before it turned back to the abdomen between its four hands. They moved like a spider admiring a bug in its web. He saw it pluck a long strand of hair from its balding head and use it to continue stitching.

"Almost done, dear…" it assured. "Don't you worry; *she's almost done."*

"ANGEL!"

Protective instincts took over. James ran at the hag, tackling it with his full weight. Needles and nightmarish tools spilled across the floor when they landed in a heap against the wall. It may have been tall but it was thin and frail. Its limbs crumpled as it wheezed from the breath being knocked from its body.

The smell was overwhelming. Death stench washed over him, and he scrambled to escape from the tangle and return to his wife. Horror met him at her side.

Angel was a grotesque sight. Ugly stitches ran up her stomach to leave it butchered and grim. A bloody gash cut through her chest over her heart to match his own. Entire patches of hair were missing from her scalp. In their place, were red splotches as if they had been ripped out by assaulting fists. Even then, nothing could compare to the state of her abdomen. It looked to have been torn down the middle with a rusty blade. A festering seam rose half an inch from the smooth plane of her surrounding skin.

Nausea did flips in James's stomach. Silent prayers ran through his mind as he knelt over her. As gentle as he dared, he tried to rouse his love and bring her back to a world certain to be hell. He lightly cradled her head and tapped her cheeks to bring her to, but his voice betrayed his fright.

"Angel? *Angel, wake up! WAKE UP!*" Hysteria forced his hands to shake. "*Oh God, what did she do to you?*"

She stirred. Angel's face contorted with returning awareness. Only for a moment did confusion occupy her mind before agony arrived.

"*AUGH!*" Her hands clutched her abdomen. Sitting forward brought forth screams of pain that rang in James's ears. Any slight movement forced recently severed core muscles to flex. Terrified eyes stared at the fissure of flesh under her fingers. "WHAT HAPPENED TO ME? I– *JAMES!*" She looked up for any form of help but only became more frightened. *"YOUR EYE!"*

"Nngh…"

The thing was stirring. A tangle of limbs and fingers stole Angel's attention. Ghastly fright turned her expression into an unnatural grimace of terror.

"WHAT IN GOD'S NAME IS THAT?"

"Oh, my dear…" it rasped, rising onto its hands. The hag crawled toward them on all six limbs. Pale eyes stared through a thin veil of hair. Cackles clacked a jaw loose on one side. *"Is that any way to say thank you?"*

James was like a deranged animal. Angel hadn't seen him grab the ax, but every fevered swing left a tearing sound of skin and bone echoing through her head. Blood sprayed from the blade to spatter across her face as terror fueled James's efforts. Even as arms and legs were separated from the hag's body, the thing laughed with a thick, gurgled enjoyment.

He hacked until the aging ax head snapped off and fell to the floor with a dull *thunk*. Breaths brought his back to rise and fall as he stood over the monster.

Tremors rattled Angel. *"James… What happened? Where are we? What is that– NGH!"*

Pain struck like lightning. Her hands flew to her stomach as her face contorted. James turned to see her abdomen pulsating under her fingers.

"Angel?"

Breathlessness left her words ghostly. "Something… is inside of me… *I can… feel it– A-AAUGH! Moving!"* She looked at her husband. Where he expected to find horror was instead a hysterical expression of joy. He had seen that expression only once before. *"I-I think I'm pregnant!"*

He was helping her to her feet within seconds. Careful to have her use her core as little as possible, James brought Angel to stand with his shoulder as a crutch. "We'll find a doctor. You're going to be alright. We'll get to the car and–"

A cackle drove a spike through their hearts. Angel's eyes widened as the pile of body parts began writhing. From the hag's exposed, bloody flesh wiggled thin threads, coiling out of her severed muscles like hidden tapeworms. They sought their missing counterparts. Pale eyes rolled in the hag's head, trained on the couple. Its laughter grew louder as one arm reattached itself. Stitches pulled and criss-crossed her body. A clawed hand reached for the other limbs to gather them into a bundle. Stitches whipped and snapped from her wounds, eager to pull themselves back together.

Angel's face contorted in the lantern light. *"JAMMMES!"*

He pulled her along. If it couldn't be killed, they had to run. Grabbing the lantern, he examined the other side of the room. A flight of stairs led down into a choking darkness. Behind them, the sickening sound of flesh scraped across the floor as the hag drug itself forward with one hand.

"Where are you going, dear?"

The dark stairway was preferable to the reassembling evil. Clutching her sutured abdomen, Angel depended on her husband for every bit of balance. Her legs had no strength to carry her alone. The stairs flew under her feet as James barreled to the lower floor. They were back in the antique shop.

"Ok, ok come on! The car is just outside!" James urged, limping Angel through the aisles.

A cascade of thuds shook the building. A severed hand and leg tumbled down the stairs behind them before the rest of the hag followed head over heels. Its tangled body tensed and grasped for any kind of purchase halfway down the stairs. Unnatural movements shifted the jumbled mass in unexpected ways. She was a pile of demonic body parts working together for locomotion, moving like a monstrous fleshy spider down the remaining steps.

"But you can't leave…! There's so much we must prepare for! The time draws close, my dear!"

She was coming back together, although nothing was returning to its rightful place. Stitches pulled her arms and legs to random points on her torso. Some of their joints conjoined, whereas others were completely missing. The squirming mass pushed James to run, but Angel stopped in her tracks.

"James! J-JAMES!" Monumental discomfort twisted her visage. *"Something is–"*

Agony pulled her gaze downward. Her hands grabbed the sides of her stomach as it pushed outward. Skin tightened and bulged between her fingers. Tension pulled at the stitches one after another.

She was getting bigger.

"OH MY GOD!"

"We don't have long, dear!" the hag called in pursuit.

Fevered slapping and clawing came from the stairs when the creature resumed pursuit. With its body so dismembered, its only form of movement was a haphazard scramble of limbs kicking and grabbing whatever they could to drag itself across the floor. Ghoulish eyes stared from the middle of the bundle.

Angel's breath bucked. Her wound seared as if on fire. Having distended several inches, her split abdomen was already beginning to strain. She followed James's lead out the front door, as scrambling claws crashed against shelves behind them.

A desolate night embraced the couple. Evening's chill stung against their sweating skin.

James's head spun on a swivel around the dirt lot. "Where's the car? *WHERE'S THE CAR?*"

It was gone. There was nothing between them and the road. A breeze whistled to rustle the ocean of corn stalks surrounding the building.

A pounding came from the door. The hag was slamming herself against the glass. Spreading cracks urged him to flee with his lover. Dried stalks, scratching each other in the wind, bid them enter and hide.

"Dear! Oh, my dear! Come back!" The hag's voice flew into the wind when her scrambling form escaped the door. Dirt crunched under her clawing hands and buckling joints. *"Don't worry! I'm coming to help you! It takes a village!"*

James didn't dare look back. Stalks whipped at his body and scratched his burning wounds with every step. It was dark in the cornfield, even with the lantern's aid. Its light hardly cast more than a few feet ahead. Stalks cracked behind them from the creature's pursuit.

"Hurry, Angel! We can make it! We just need to hide!"

Her hand tightened in response. Blood dripped from her belly as it tightened against her palm. Pained groans betrayed her overwhelming agony from stitches pulling at drum-tight skin. "It's growing! Oh, James! *Look at me!*" Maniacal giggle fits mixed with her terrified gasps. If James didn't know better, he would have thought Angel was happy. "*I must be six months pregnant!*"

"Listen to me! *You're not pregnant! This isn't real!* This is a nightmare! You can't be–"

He dared to look. Angel was indeed distending dangerously large. Stretch marks were shooting over her girth. In the waving shadows of the corn, her stomach seemed to lurch and pulse with a mind of its own. Something wanted out. Micro tears were splitting open around the stitches to create fresh rivulets of blood.

"*Augh!*" Angel agonized, her free hand clawing at her growth. Her steps were slowing. Poor balance and mind-blurring pain threatened to take her to the ground. "*It hurts!*"

"*We can't stop! We need to–*" James looked around. There were no landmarks. Nothing visible over the corn. Even the shop was out of sight. They were lost in a sea of beige and blackness, afloat with only their lantern as his wife neared bursting.

"*Come back, my dear…! You'll need help!*"

The hag's voice seemed to come from every direction. They might have been lost, but it knew exactly where they were.

Angel's legs gave out. Her knees fell into the tilled dirt and she released James's hand in favor of cradling her stomach. Wide eyes stared at the gore decorating her front, like a lightning bolt gleaming red in the lantern light. The fleshy seam dividing her gut looked ready to burst open.

"James! *James, look at me!*" Angel laughed and admired herself. Madness filled her bloodshot eyes. There was no room for fear in her mind, not when there was such a soul-swallowing abyss aching to be filled. *"I-I'm so much further along than last time!"*

"GET UP!"

His voice was meaner and more demanding than he'd meant it to be. Remorse panged his heart immediately after. Moisture shined Angel's eyes and her lips trembled with sadness.

"Don't… D-Don't you want this…?" Tears ran down her face as she began to sob. She held her widening belly. *"Isn't this what we both wanted?"*

"Not–" James held his tongue. He didn't want his panic to break his wife's heart. "Not… *this.*"

"B-But what does it matter if–"

A cackling voice gurgling with oil came from behind her. *"Let me see how my seams are doing, my dear…"* Spidery fingers emerged from the darkness to curl around corn stalks for support. Glowing pale eyes followed from within a creeping mass of limbs. Blackened teeth smiled as a hand reached to grasp Angel's shoulder.

Her shriek pierced the night sky. Light flashed. Before James knew what he was doing, the lantern had already been thrown at the monstrosity. Flames burst around the hag. Oil spilled and caught fire to her body and surrounding corn. What was once a little flame, rapidly matured into a full-fledged bonfire.

"Aaahhrreeaaahhhh!"

The hag's screams were nails being hammered into James's brain. Taking his wife by the arm, he pulled her up and raced deeper into the field. Crackling flames and screams chased after them. Stalks shattered at the hag's thrashing to subdue the blaze but it was spreading too fast.

Soon, its shrieks faded away in the distance. In their place, came blood-chilling laughter behind James's back. He pulled her along in delicate panic; visions of her belly's jostling contents proving too heavy for its seams, blurred through his mind.

Angel was hysterical, frenzied with desperate love and desire. James pulled but she wouldn't follow. Her steps slowed to a pregnant halt. Around them, the night was glowing with firelight. The blaze was spreading to engulf the field. James could have been fooled into thinking the sun was rising if the smell of smoke wasn't burning his sinuses so badly.

"James… James… This is it." Angel's chest heaved with unbridled joy. She gazed at the stitch-wrapped gift between her hands. It throbbed with a tightness that was ready to split open, like a reddened ripe fruit. The pain didn't matter.

"We can't stop! WE CAN'T STOP, ANGEL!"

He looked to her for any sign of sanity but found only glazed eyes. Angel's belly had reached its fullest. Flames reflected across her overstretched skin. The stitches could barely hold her suture together. Rising orange glows danced across her disfigured body. Saucer-sized eyes trembled with madness.

Angel struggled for breath. Nails dug into her belly to split deep gouges and draw blood. *"James… I can feel… Nnngh!"*

Her stomach heaved and bucked. Something kicked hard enough to tear several stitches open. Still, Angel stared in crazed affection. In the distance, a hag's laugh drifted over the fire.

"The… contractions! It's happening! IT'S FINALLY HAPPENING! She's coming! *SHE'S COMING, JAMES! Our little girl!*"

James couldn't look away even as her pulsating abdomen looked ready to rip open and spill across the ground. Angel's stance spread wider. A gush of fluid and blood fell out of her, turning the dirt into mud. In the flickering light, James could see a dozen strands of thread swaying between her legs like loose puppet strings.

Screaming in joyful agony, Angel announced, "I'M GOING TO BE A *MOTHER!*"

She fell backward to land with her legs spread before James. Leaning up on her arms, she pleaded with her husband, "Catch our daughter! She's coming! *Catch our baby girl!*"

James knew only horror could be delivered. There would be no true happiness in whatever she birthed. He knelt before her, extending his hands. His eyes couldn't bear to look away even as his instincts told him to flee.

"*Aaaauuuugh! AHHH!*"

Blood flowed and her body heaved. Angel's screams blanketed the night. The bellows of a woman in labor overpowered the fire.

James prayed whatever was about to happen would be over soon.

"*AAAHHHHH!*"

Her mouth stretched into an unnatural silent scream, threatening to dislocate her jaw. All noise fell away when a flood poured over James's hands.

Something solid slid into his outstretched grasp.

Angel collapsed. Relief had come. Dramatic breaths

filled her lungs, one after another with smoke. She couldn't hear anything over her own heartbeat pounding in her ears. Once tight enough to rupture, her belly and stitches had loosened like a deflated balloon, leaving the mound sagging over her abdomen.

Weak, she raised her eyes. Her voice was weak and little more than a whimper. *"James... James, let me see... Let me see our girl..."*

Horror enveloped his face. The crying started slowly but rose into a horrid screech. Out of everything they had been through tonight, this wailing was by far the worst.

He shook his head. "Angel..."

Pleading filled her eyes. She held out a hand and started to sob. *"L-Let me see...!"*

"I don't think–"

"LET ME SEE MY BABY!"

Months of grief fermented the demand into a shriek of desperation. James's heart broke as he realized he had no choice. As the fire spread around them, he approached his wife's side and placed their child in her shaking arms. There was no umbilical cord.

A cackle danced over the blaze.

Angel watched as a grotesque abomination entered her embrace. A horrific abhorrence, not meant for mortal eyes. Disfigurement assailed the infant on all fronts. Within a ribcage far too small, beat a heart several sizes too large. Every pulse strained the flesh to the point of tearing. Its left hand was missing, sutured into a bloody stub. The other was a crude amalgamation of James's missing fingers. They sat sewn to the end of a doll's arm, complete with a blue bracelet. Its thighs were melded together into a single piece of flesh, more closely resembling a seal than a human infant. Stitches and seams ran over its joints and skin in a makeshift attempt to hold everything together. The head was malformed like a rotting melon. Patches of hair had been haphazardly sewn into the scalp. One oversized eye was ready to pop free of its socket.

There was no humanity in its cries. Its wails were ghoulish and cursed. Every shrill tone wore at their souls.

Angel stared at James with watering eyes. A broken smile, waiting for a punchline to her grief, wavered with whispered insanity. *"Where… Where is my daughter, James…? T- This isn't my daughter…"*

"Oohhhhh what a beautiful girl…!" a voice prattled. From the blazing stalks, emerged the hag's melted spidery form. The cackle energized into a laugh and her gaze fell upon James and his stitched socket burned. *"She's got your eye!"*

Angel's mind had broken. Her heart ached for a demented horror her mind could never let her love. This was not her child. This was not what she was promised.

Mind reeling, she tried to drop the thing. Stitches and thread sprang from the child like worms to burrow themselves into her hands and arms.

"No! This– *This is not mine!*"

She ripped herself free of the threads and tried once more to push the thing away. More stitches sprouted from its body, reeling it in close. All the while, its howling grew to a deafening level.

"NO! THIS ISN'T MINE! THIS ISN'T MY GIRL!"

Angel ripped and pulled. Blood poured from her torn skin in her effort to rid herself of the thing. The attachment couldn't be severed no matter how many filaments she tore.

James felt numb. Limp. The wails were too much. As the

fire grew, encircling them in the corn, he watched Angel collapse onto her back. Fresh grief filled her sobbing shrieks. She flailed, powerless to rid herself of the horror crawling over her body to search for her breasts. Only when it latched did the wailing finally cease. Blood trickled from the corner of its lipless mouth. Angel clawed at her tear-streamed face. Renewed heartbreak and anguish filled the air with her screams as the child's threads dug into her torso, securing itself in place.

Fire roared as smoke burned their lungs and tongues flame licked their bodies. Cackles drifted from the encroaching inferno as James sat slumped helplessly next to his wife. Blood-soaked wounds hissed in the heat. Searching at his side, Jame's hand found Angel's and squeezed.

The encroaching blaze was nothing compared to her miserable wails.

"You make a lovely family…"

About *Patchwork*

What can I say about this one? It's gross. It's gory. It's a nightmarish, twisted, monkey's paw of a story. Those were all hopes for it, at least. At some point in writing this anthology, I set a goal to write something truly horrific. That's where Patchwork *came from: just me trying to push my limits. It was also an instance where the title came first and worked backward from there. I played with a few ideas, but eventually landed on the patchwork hag and this poor couple trying to regain what they'd lost.*

Is this a story about finding peace? Letting go? Regret? Something about how much parents sacrifice for their children? I don't know. At the very least, I think it's a story about what grief can drive a person to do in pursuit of what they've lost. And that sometimes, it's better to let the lost stay lost.

About the Author

David Corisis is a born-and-raised Idahoan and graduate of Gonzaga University's School of Computer Science. He lives the exciting life of a programmer by day and aspiring writer by night. When not sharing a keyboard with his cat, David enjoys running, brewing mead, playing video games, camping, frustrating his friends with Piranha Plant in Super Smash Bros., and worrying about the ever-marching hand of time stealing everything he holds dear. His favorite books include *At the Mountains of Madness*, and *Flatland*. He couldn't be happier taking on the world and its challenges with his undeserved wife at his side.

You can follow David at dcorisis.com or @dcorisis.

About the Illustrator

Sara Vasquez is a Chicana illustrator and designer whose distinctive style brings stories to life. When not partaking in the daily PNW activities of sparkling in a rare sunbeam, stalking through the woods, or crawling out of a well, she can be found petting neighborhood cats, gathering herbs, and indulging in a good cackle. Her major influences include Mexican folk art, local flora and fauna, and comics. She credits her wonderful family, partner, and friends for embracing her weirdness.

See more good stuff or get in contact at hellosara.me and @sarita.draws

www.ingramcontent.com/pod-product-compliance
Lightning Source LLC
Chambersburg PA
CBHW031536310726

48971CB00008B/2507